Auction of Worlds

By

Carl S. Kralich

Auction of Worlds

By
Carl S. Kralich

Published by Ruskras Corner
The United States of America

Auction of Worlds - A Karl Sabers Space Knight Adventure
By Carl S. Kralich
ISBN 9781942542155

Second in a series

The Universe of the Mid 3700s

See the Galactic Guide
Page 128

Cast of Characters

Crew of the *Nemesis, Starlight* and *Lady Eris*

Karl Sabers- A former student from the colony ship *Nomad,* he is now the captain of group of space privateers in service to Sophia and her quest to restore the empire that conquered Earth.

Sophia Rubyeyes- The alien princess of the fallen Neith Empire. She seeks to find her missing sister and place her on the throne. Her ability to run Karl's life is second only to Lightening.

Lightening- Chatty cat rules with an iron paw, easily bribed with tuna.

Calidi- The elder of Sophia's royal guard, he disapproves of her association with a Terran man. Disapproves of Zrela.

Ellris- The younger of Sophia's royal guard, Calidi's apprentice.

Alice- A young mechanic from Ganymede who was recruited by the pirates when her previous ship was commandeered.

Reginia- A strange Koal woman serving as a fighter in Karl's crew.

Henry Hunter- A soldier turned pirate from the totalitarian moon Io.

Miss Holo- A tactical AI that was reprogrammed into a virtual teacher, in times of peace she misses her power in the classroom.

Gavin Hager- Karl's main engineer, prone to rogue tampering.

Zrela- A Neith commoner who is known for dressing like a Terran.

Justin- Son of a grand councilor, loyalty is his trademark.

Jacob- Son of a supreme court judge, now part of Karl's crew.

Oracle- An alien artifact of undetermined origin who used Karl Sabers to escape from the Evlon sect. He can do no harm.

Crew of the *Crimson Blade*

Denise- Karl’s younger evangelical sister, serving as cook on the *Crimson Blade.* Her personal missions- wed Surge, act as his food warden, and convert the entire galaxy to Christianity.

Surge- Half-alien bounty hunter and commander of the *Crimson Blade.* He mixes foods that should never be in the same room.

Ray- Mechanic for the *Crimson Blade,* also the ship's CFO, he keeps the engines running and imposes his miserly habits on all.

B10- A Gynoid navigation unit, believes in the inferiority of organics.

Kira- A young Lrakian bounty hunter on the *Crimson Blade.*

Inhabitants of the Galaxy

Charles Sanwell- Creator of the Auction of Worlds, he hopes the event will bring unlimited wealth and power to himself.

Ashley Claymore- An old merchant working behind the auction scene, he shanghais anyone available and sells them for cash.

Baldassara- One of the lords of the Syndicate. As Sophia's uncle, he seeks to restore the Neith monarchy by any means necessary.

Prince Alec- Fourteenth in line to the Throne of the Titan Empire, his mission is managing and defending a new colony world.

Prince Ulai- Handsome ruler of the Principality of Talon, a former vassal to the Neith Empire in charge of a colony star system.

Father Abraham- Sent to the auction by the Mars Vatican, he wants to make a sacrifice to wake up the world to the evil in the galaxy.

Father Gabriel- A half-alien assistant to Father Abraham, he is a source of refuge to all species regardless of planet or origin.

Kordova- A representative of the Evlon sect, he once controlled the Oracle. He wants it back and he will be at the auction.

Narkren- Grand Protector of the Neith Federation. In constant fear of a return to power by the monarchy, he deals harshly with political dissidents. No one wants to cross him.

Admiral Dalia- A Madam Admiral of the Neith Federation. Unwilling to admit defeat, she destroys every object in range as she retreats. Her next diabolical mission takes her to the auction.

King Bob- A Lrakian pride leader, owner of the underground casino where the auction bidders come to gamble for cash..

Yuki Amato- An innocent refugee from the Koal attack on the Nomad, she is now up for auction to the highest bidder.

Brittany- one of Denise's friend and former classmates from the *Nomad,* her life has changed drastically since the attack.

John Madison- One of Karl's friends and former classmates from the *Nomad* who assisted in resisting the Koal attack.

Travis Bowie Crockett- Another of Karl's former classmates from the *Nomad,* named after the Alamo heroes of ancient Earth.

Isabella- Claymore's faithful Lrakian servant. Her role is to stand by and be available to assist her conniving master.

Table of Contents

Chapter 1- The Formidable Admiral

"How dare they!" Fleet Admiral Dalia kicked her heel against the base stem of her chair. "I'll crush them completely."

The admiral's eyes glanced at the shattering of a small Neith frigate before looking over at one of the Terran vessels. A beam from Dalia's flagship penetrated the Terran ship's hull, causing the core of the enemy ship to detonate, leaving a burnout husk.

"Admiral," said a copper haired Lecaran officer. "Orders from First Protector Narkren, we are to withdraw from this battle at once."

"WHAT!" yelled the admiral, rising from her seat.

The admiral was dressed in a feminine uniform, a knee length trim blue dress with long sleeves ending in black cuffs, matching her high collar. Her silver hair was already starting to blacken.

Her allegiance to Cralton, a great floating city of Venus, motivated her every action.

Venus, which the Lecarans had taken as their capital world, was the most important planet of the Neith Federation. Moreover, it was her home and she felt the threat to her world in her soul.

She had to put down this rebellion by the Lunar Confederacy.

"If we don't crush them now, another stronghold will stand as an enemy of the federation."

"Admiral Dalia." The voice of Jarl Narkren broadcast across the bridge. "You have your orders. Withdraw immediately."

"Understood," she growled before switching off. "Begin the drop!"

"But Admiral! Our orders?" The first officer tossed his arms up.

"Rest assured, we are pulling out as ordered."

As the fleet of gold and black ships fell back, a gigantic asteroid raced towards the moon.

The Lunar fleet opened fire in an attempt to destroy the lump of iron and rock.

The asteroid shattered a raining hail of debris upon Lunar cities below.

Chapter 2- Princesses, Pirates, and Cats

In a different star system far away, a four-legged creature covered in yellow-orange fur made its way down the steel gray hallway of the abandoned asteroid mining base.

The pointed ears twitched, the slit-like pupils having spotted an open air vent. Making its way down the air duct, the creature arrived at a vent cover overlooking an office with two humanoids.

"Do you realize the consequences of what you did?" A young alien woman in a short black dress ran her white gloved fingers through her long metallic gold hair. Her ruby red irises were fixed on a young Terran.

"I'm sorry, I didn't mean to upset you," replied the man. "But this is completely necessary. I mean it's not like…"

At that very moment the grate covering the air duct popped open and the cat flew towards the young man. The man reached out his arms grabbing the animal, who immediately sunk its claws into the man's waistcoat and climbed up towards the man's head.

"Lightening, what have I told you?" he asked the purring feline, now perched on his shoulder.

"I'm just so happy to see you, Karl," said the tomcat, nuzzling the man's light brown hair. "Also, I haven't been fed in weeks."

"He's lying." Sophia crossed her arms. "I fed him this morning."

"Would I lie to you?" Lightening rubbed his face against Karl's.

Karl looked at Lightening, then glanced back at Sophia. "You'll have to wait for…"

He stopped talking as his handheld beeped. He stared at the image of a holographic AI.

"Yes?"

"I have come to educate you on current affairs."

"Not now, Miss Holo! We're in the middle of-"

"This is important, Karl Sabers. An important battle is underway at this moment near earth."

"So what? I'm busy here."

Sophia crossed her arms and tapped her glass slippered toes

impatiently.

"This is a battle where the Luna Confederacy is trying to gain independence from the Neith Federation. As you recall, following the execution of the royal family-"

Karl snapped his handheld off. A historical lesson did not fit his mood right now, despite his love of history.

His present life demanded his attention.

The female wearing the frosted glass slippers and a small black dress filled his mind completely until...

A knock on the door sounded sharply.

Sophia pushed a button and the panel slid open.

A middle-aged Lecaran man entered the room, his gold hair partially blackened with age.

"Lady Ver… Sophia, Captain Sabers, I have the names you requested." The alien man pulled out a round black disc-like device. This object had a transparent orange rim around it in a crystal center. Karl drew a similar device from within his waistcoat and the data transferred between the handheld computers.

"Thanks." Karl placed the object back in his pocket. "By the way, why didn't you just transfer the data wirelessly?"

"As acting head of the royal guard, it is my duty to personally ensure the safety of Her Highness while in exile," he answered.

"Head of all two royal guards," Lightening added.

"Cat!" Sophia snapped, glaring at the feline before turning back to her subordinate. "You are dismissed, Calidi."

"Yes, Your Highness." Calidi bowed before Sophia, before his yellow irises sent a glare at Karl. The guardsmen then turned and left the room.

Doing his best to ignore Calidi's distaste, Karl returned to the matter at hand.

"*Prometheus, Enterprise*," Karl began, reading aloud a list on his handheld. "*Roswell, Nirvana, Ruby Eyed Empress, Nemesis, Serenity, Veris, Sargoth Veris, the Sargoth's Revenge,* and *His Holiness Emperor of the Known Universe, the Iron Paw Lightening*."

Sophia and Karl's eyes rolled towards Lightening.

"I like the last one." The feline smirked.

"Well, what do you think?" Karl deleted the last entry on the list before turning to Sophia.

"I don't see why we need to change the name of the ship in the first place," she commented. "However, having the ship named after myself does seem to have appeal."

"I thought you wanted to keep your real name a secret?" Karl reminded her.

"You're right. I guess *Nemesis* sounds the most interesting." Sophia pulled a silvery cape off her chair and wrapped her bare shoulders. "Do I make the announcement on the bridge?"

With the feline still on his right shoulder, Karl picked up his blazer and slung over it his left arm. He then left with the alien girl and the cat, heading towards a lift.

Karl smiled upon seeing the stolen black and gold frigate. A far more impressive looking ship than any of the Terran ships due to her golden bow, constructed like a split arrowhead and stern-mounted rear swept wings.

Docked beside the frigate was a smaller crimson ship with a diamond shaped bow and a slender hull section with a pair of curved wings on either side of the ship.

The elevator lowered automatically to a covered gangplank leading to the frigate. Karl Sabers followed Sophia into the bronze corridor lined with crystal pillars.

They passed by three humanoids who stood looking at a floating gold disc with a spherical crystal center.

Four diamond shaped gems orbited the rim of the disk. A pair of crystals hovered at the top and bottom of the object.

"Are you designed for repair?" An Asian boy in his early teens looked up at the floating saucer. He held in his right hand a sickle sword with a brass knuckle guard.

"No data is available at this time," the object replied.

"So, were you built for combat?" asked a slightly younger girl with pointed catlike ears and a long white tail coming from under her dress.

"I am programmed not to harm organics," the disc answered.

"I fail to see the purpose of a self-aware, artificial intelligence that cannot defend itself," opined the monotone voice of a slender black haired girl in a skintight black jumpsuit.

"So you want a robot rebellion." Lightening rolled on the cool floor and began nuzzling Karl’s shoe. "I would prefer that the machines not declare you humans obsolete. We cats would lose all those generations of work we put into training humans if you were exterminated."

"That is why my creator's race programmed me with the three laws," the machine replied.

"And what are those?" The boy rested the sheathed weapon on his shoulder.

"The first law- machine should never bring harm to an intelligent lifeform, and the third law is that a machine must protect itself unless it violates the first or second law," said the floating disc.

"Oracle, you left out the second one." Lightening wiped his face. "What is it?"

"Second law..." The crystals orbiting the Oracle disc turned green. "Error. Not found. I seem to be missing data in that section. Maybe it will come to me later."

"You are a machine. If the data is not there now, it doesn't exist anymore." Ray ran his fingers through his black hair.

"You're a very pessimistic human." The floating crystal turned clear again. "I thought youth was supposed to be full of hope and optimism."

A ring came from a device in the boy's pocket.

"Kira, Ray, I need you back on the *Crimson Blade*," a voice from the device commanded. "We'll be leaving soon."

The cat-eared girl and the boy turned to leave, while the black haired woman remained a moment with Karl, Sophia, Lightening and the floating disc.

"B-10, are you coming?" Ray directed his question to the black haired woman.

"Surge did not call for me," the gynoid replied. "And you have not yet returned Captain Sabers' weapon."

"Right." Ray handed the sickle sword to Karl. "I'm so used to fixing Surge's weapons that I forgot it was yours."

Karl pulled the khopesh from its sheath revealing the glass blade.

A thin diagonal line of transparent gold now marked the transition from the straight unsharpened ricasso to the sudden dropping curve of the cutting edge.

He smiled at the restoration of his weapon.

Karl claimed the sword of a fallen assassin as his own, his life having become entangled in constant danger after meeting Sophia.

The khopesh was one of his most prized possessions.

"Thanks." Karl strapped the weapon to his belt. "Oracle, I'll need you on the bridge."

They passed through the doorway onto the bridge, which appeared to be almost completely open to the stars, excepting chairs and holographic computer panels. Karl looked around the 360 degree display of the universe surrounding the ship.

It's mine, Karl thought with a smirk. He sank down in the captain's chair in the center of the bridge.

Chapter 3- A Pivotal Battle

Beams of yellow and purple streaked across the sky of the former homeworld of humanity. A planet now stained with the purple vegetation of her conquers. Broadsided by a fleet of gold and black Neith warships, with split arrowhead shaped bows, was a fleet consisting half of the same class of ships, repainted silver and white, plus other ships which were obsolete warships of Mars and Titan.

The admiral's flagship fired fifty beams from her starboard side into a frigate, tearing through the white ship's shields.

"We have to continue firing until we can escape to Venus!" Admiral Dalia commanded.

"We're doing the best we can!" An officer yelled just as a direct hit jerked him off his feet.

"Your best is not good enough!" screamed the admiral. "They are chasing us!"

Volleys of missiles launched from the Martian and Titan-built ships, as swarms of drones surrounded the Neith warships firing smaller beams at any warhead that got close.

The Neith ships turned to broadside the Lunar rebels.

Six rebel ships prepared their railguns, each blasting a single projectile from stern to bow, aiming at a single gold and black vessel, shredding her against the blackness of space.

A dozen frigates and two Neith cruisers broadsided the Lunar warships before they could fire again.

"How far do they intend to follow us?"

No one replied.

They were busy.

The mere idea of being ordered to retreat made Dalia's skin crawl. Then she controlled herself-

At least I can take a few more of them down along the way home.

A pair of missiles flew by the drones of a warship a few miles from the admiral's flagship. The missiles detonated inside the Neith cruiser, leaving just a smoking husk to burn away in Earth's atmosphere.

"Admiral, the orbital patrol fleet will be in range in-"

The flagship jolted with the detonation from a warhead striking her shields.

"Find which ship launched that warhead." She strangled the armrest with her left hand. "Fire all port side guns at that vessel and make sure there is nothing left."

The already crumbling Lunar dreadnought was torn apart by fifty simultaneous particle beams.

The old empire never should have left red bloods outside their rule to rise up against us. Now we have to deal with these traitors on Luna.

She watched the holographic display of the two fleets around her. Slowly a ship of the same class as Dalia's came upon her, planted in the colors of the Luna Confederacy.

Which admiral allowed such a disgrace as to allow their own flagship to become a tool of traitors?

As the two capital ships blasted away each other's guns, a small fleet of undamaged Neith cruisers from Earth's orbit fired upon Dalia's enemy.

The Lunar flagship shattered from the particle beams coming from all sides.

With their commanders dead, the pursuing fleet abandoned the chase as the broken flotilla sank into the gravity well of Earth.

"Have a list of all the fallen ready for me in my quarters, along with the actions leading up to their deaths." Dalia rose from her seat and left to prepare the memorial documents for each of those lost under her command.

"This battle is over."

Chapter 4- The Auction is Announced

"Karl Sabers, you need to pay attention to what I am trying to teach you. You know that when you neglect what I say-"

"I know. Bad things happen." Karl completed Miss Holo's thought as he once again aborted her attempt to intervene via the handheld.

It had been less than a year since Karl Sabers had been taken from the *Nomad*, the generational ship on which he was born.

Now, after an attempt to rescue his sister from alien slavers had led him to Sophia, he felt he was completely adjusted to a galaxy, which he had not even known existed a year ago.

"Attention crew of the newly christened *Nemesis*," the captain announced. "Set course for the rendezvous point."

I wonder if I should get someone out there in a spacesuit and Christen the ship properly with a bottle of wine. But how would we get the bottle to break? A wine cannon?

The holographic AI appeared, programmed to resemble a woman in glasses with a pale blue dress suit projected over her.

"You cannot escape me by turning off your handheld. You forget I am programmed to appear before you whenever my bots detect a problem with you, Captain."

"I wish you were programmed to do that whenever he forgets to feed me exactly the cuisine I deserve." Lightening licked his fangs.

"Shut up, cat. You do not compute with me."

"I recall delivering you to the Koal mothership's bridge during the attack on the Nomad last year."

"As far as I am concerned, you were merely functioning as a transport device. I was created by humans, humans have used animals as transport devices almost exclusively until 20th century Earth when they were replace by mechanized device, except train travel did begin earlier in the-"

"Miss Holo! What are you doing here? Please relay your message," Karl demanded with exasperation.

"There is a shuttle returning from the *Crimson Blade*," the holographic woman informed. "Now about the battle- "

"That's enough, Miss Holo. Please disappear now."

Miss Holo vanished as quickly as she came.

A small gray shuttle from the red ship made her way towards the *Nemesis*.

The shuttle slipped into the main hanger of the frigate. A few moments later a man in his mid-twenties with metallic copper hair and a teenage girl with olive skin walked onto the bridge escorted by Calidi along with a younger member of his race.

Surge, a skilled bounty hunter, was the copper haired man. He wore a faded long coat with tarnished triangular buckles. At his side was a katana with a dragon hilt that matched his hair color. Marking the man as a halfbreed were his blue Terran eyes.

The olive skinned girl was Karl's sister, Denise. Her encounter with alien slavers over a year ago left her basically unchanged. She was still stubborn and arrogant. Despite their different skin tones, the two siblings had the same green eyes.

"I thought you two were off to find my sister, Vlora?" Sophia hoped something might have been discovered.

"You humans seem to forget something every time you go on a trip," Lightening observed.

"Lightening, I did not forget anything." Denise looked down at Lightening. "Ray thinks that we might have discovered a possible location for the princess."

"Where?" Karl jumped from his seat as alarms sound.

"Neith scoutship detected! Repeat! Neith scoutship detected!" came over the intercom.

"Oh, what now? Raise shields!" Karl ordered, sitting down in his chair. "How did they find us?"

A small diamond shaped vessel, with forward swept wings, appeared from a starless pocket of space. The spacecraft was black with gold trim.

An artificial intelligence, once just a tactical AI teacher, now repurposed as a Holographic security consultant, Miss Holo often exhibited motherly overtones towards her ex-students.

These included Karl and Denise, along with crew members, Justin and Jacob, among others aboard.

"We don't know." Miss Holo popped up on Karl's handheld,

while tracking the craft with the *Nemesis'* ray-turrets. "We're not picking up life signs."

A figure of a man popped up on the wall. He had dark black hair and a thin mustache. He stood about six feet two. He was dressed in a black sports coat, with black jeans and cowboy boots.

A cowboy? Karl thought to himself. *He's missing his hat. Does he have a Peacemaker?*

"Hello. I am Charles Sanwell." A circle of small gavels began orbiting him. "You are invited-"

The sound of footsteps interrupted the man.

"Hey, Charles?" A female voice called out. "Some of the guys were wondering..." The voice paused for a second. "Hey! Are you doing the thing now?"

"Yeah," the man said. "Goodbye."

"Rude..." The female voice muttered. Then she spoke again. "To the people who are getting this. Hi! And I hope I see you at the auction!"

Then they heard the woman's footsteps fading away.

"As I was saying," the man known as Charles began again. "You are invited to the Auction of Worlds. This is the address." He pointed to six constellations that appeared right next to him. The man pulled a gold watch out of his pocket. "You have one minute to copy these down." Charles raised his hand. "Sayonara." Then he disappeared, leaving the symbols behind.

"Got any idea what he's talking about?" Karl spun his chair towards his crewmen.

"I don't know. I have never heard of this Charles Sanwell or his Auction of Worlds," Calidi answered.

"We-" Denise turned back to the others.

Once again, a hologram of the same man appeared in front of them. "The auction will start two weeks from today, and will last four days," he informed them. Then the hologram disappeared.

"At least we know when it starts." Lightening wiped his face with his paw.

About a minute or two after the symbols disappeared, the scoutship left with the *Nemesis*' guns still tracking the vessel until it left normal space.

"Enough of this distraction." Sophia stomped her foot making a ding as the glass struck metal. "What did he find about my sister?"

"How did your shoe not break?" Denise crouched down to look at Sophia's shoes which were undamaged. "And how do you even walk in them?"

Sophia stepped back.

"Their woven fibers of the same glass as my sword." Karl pulled his khopesh from its scabbard. "So it would take at least a charge-cutter to damage them."

"There's also a set of hinges built into the sole so I can walk in them." Sophia looked down at Denise. "They are also available in sapphire or emerald and metallic such as gold and silver. If you are that interested, I'm sure you can find a pair on the black market or have a set custom printed. Now if we're done talking about my shoes, can we get back to my sister?"

"Well, there was a name that came up in our search." Denise stood back up. "It was Sanwell. The rumor is that a lost royal guest will appear."

"Great, I'll go see if Ray can find out more about this 'Auction of Worlds' thing." Surge walked out of the room.

"I guess we're going to the auction." Lightening licked his lips. "I wonder if they have any rare and valuable cat food."

"We're going to need funds for this venture," Sophia added, twisting her finger through her shiny hair. "Unless you're planning on committing acts of piracy."

"Remember we're privateers now." Karl reminded her of their letter of marque. "I'm not attacking any ships or bases unless Your Highness gives the order. And right now I would assume that you don't want to make any more enemies."

"Well, when I contacted my uncle, he advised meeting up with that gambling ring that the late Captain Micalo was allied with." Sophia smiled. "So, I guess this means making a trip back to Tau Ceti."

"So you're using this as an excuse to have a romantic rendezvous at the place where you two met." Lightening stretched his front legs. "But somehow I don't think it'll become complete unless you have her in a casket after awaking her with a kiss. You even still own the slave ship that she was on. *The Starlight.* A classy name that you will undoubtedly change."

Sophia's eyes widened as she stared at Karl.

"Is that how it went down when we first met?"

"That didn't happen! I did nothing before you woke up. Tell her." Karl looked around the room for Lightening, but he had snuck off to prowl the ship.

Chapter 5- The Haunting Past

Half-asleep and surrounded by the ornate bronze and crystal decor of her people, Sophia could not help but remember…

Running down a bronze corridor lined with pillars of crystal...

Horrified...

Her beautiful gown now tattered and stained with yellow blood...

The burnt remains of her sleeve touching the bandage just below her shoulder covering the stub of her left arm...

Behind her, the marching sound of her pursuers...

Her right heel snapping off...

Stumbling over, unable to catch her breath from the constant running…

Something damp brushing against her head like wet Velcro...

She looked up to see a pair of green eyes surrounded by a face of yellow orange fur.

Her right hand grabbed the back of the neck belonging to the creature standing on her pillow.

She lifted the longhaired tabby, bringing the feline eye level as she rose.

"What do you think you're doing?" She pointed to the Terran man sleeping in the bed on the other side of the captain's quarters with her mechanical left hand. "You belong over there."

"You humanoids only bathe once or twice a day, and you females seem to go days without washing your hair." The tomcat kicked trying to grab something with his hind legs. "I was only doing my duty of cleaning those in my care."

She tossed the cat across the room and he landed paws down on top of the sleeping young man.

"OW! LIGHTENING!"

The human bounced to life as the cat's claws sank into his stomach.

"It's Sophia's fault, I'm innocent." Lightening climbed up on the brown haired man's shoulder and began rubbing his face against

Karl's cheek.

"Well, Karl, who are you going to believe?" Sophia crossed her arms.

"I'm not getting involved in this one."

Karl considered the dispute between the alien and the cat to be more trouble than it was worth.

"We have plenty of room. Maybe we should move the cat out?" Sophia suggested.

"It would make more sense for you or Karl to move out."

"No." Sophia slapped her pillow. "I need him with me. We've also established the middle ground between our peoples' moral codes means there is nothing indecent about sharing a cabin as long we use separate beds."

"I'm feeling nostalgic for the old days where I could just be knocked out by someone and everything would be fixed when I woke up," said Karl.

Sophia looked down at her exposed mechanical forearm. The upper part of her prosthetic arm was still covered by the artificial skin with a silver band just below her shoulder, dividing her organic tissue from the synthetic covering.

It still feels numb. She lost her left arm the day her family faced a firing squad. The same family that conquered Earth paid a harsh penalty.

"Are you ever going to get it fixed?" Karl remembered the arm being a near perfect replica before the damage it sustained during their battle with an Evlon inquisitor.

"The last time I had it fixed for minor damage, I had to go without an arm for a very long night and it came back with upgrades that I didn't ask for. Who knows how long it will take this time?"

Sophia shifted her gaze to the gold slave bracelet still embedded in her right wrist. It was a reminder of the past when she had been tossed into a stasis casket and locked away for several years. While her control bracelet had been deactivated, with no light visible from the blue gem in the center, the surgery to remove it might temporally leave her without the use of her remaining hand.

She sat up and slipped on her frosted glass shoes, constructed from fibers of the same near indestructible material as Karl's sword.

She pulled on another black dress just longer than her short nightgown before fastening a gold chain around her waist.

Sophia left the cabin and Karl quickly dressed and followed. They walked down the corridor towards a cabin.

Converted into a workshop, it belonged to Gavin Hager, the mechanic of their previous ship, the *Lady Eris*.

Sophia and Karl looked over the chamber packed with broken or dismantled robots and small parts of machines.

Mixed in among the clutter were crystal-infused pieces of technology giving off the impression of value. However, most of the stuff was plastic or metals likes steel, bronze, and a black alien metal, the name of which slipped Karl's memory.

"Why did he bring all this junk?" Sophia hoped the mess would not spill over into the rest of the ship.

"This was all I could salvage after that traitor blew up the ship." A voice came from behind a stack of parts.

A young man of Terran descent with a red monocle emerged from behind a small cockpit, which appeared to have ripped from an unknown craft.

How much more did you have? Karl looked at the wall-to-wall junkyard.

"You fixed up my arm before," Sophia held out her mechanical arm. "Could you get it taken care of before we get to Tau Ceti?"

"It's going to take a little more than just reconnecting synthetic tissue this time." Gavin examined the exposed skeletal hand. "Everything, with the exception of the cybernetic skeleton below the elbow, was a total loss. We'll have to reprint the both the muscle and the dermal layers over the original frame."

"How long will that take?" Her prosthetic hand twitched.

"The arm was equipped with pigment processor and the artificial muscle fibers were able to run directly off your body's natural electric current." Gavin adjusted his monocle. "The B-10 gynoid series had a similar construction, with mechanical skeleton overlaid with synthetic flesh."

"You mean like the ancient stories of robots that are designed to infiltrate humans and assassinate their leaders?" Sophia remembered some of the ancient videos Karl had shown her.

"You're mixing legends and movies." Lightening walked along rubbing himself against each person's legs. "Not everything Karl watches is a historical document."

"In the cases like this arm, and gynoids such as B-10, the synthetics do not contain a cellular structure, and as a result cannot self-repair," Gavin explained. "With the resources on the ship, it'll take about a week for the atomic printer to reskin the arm."

"I can't be without an arm that long!" She stepped back gripping her upper left arm with her right hand.

"I have good news in that regard." Gavin began arranging a set of cybernetic arms, the first of which looked like that of a vinyl doll and the second one was metal with exposed ball joints on elbow and fingers.

"The first two are your standard prosthetic limbs. They'll cover basic function, but lack sensory capability." The next one looked like a black gantlet with blade like fingers. The fourth arm was far more ornate with frosted glass covering the brass inner workings. "And these are some custom prosthesis we happened to acquire."

The claw would make me look too much like my ancestor, she thought. *Looking like the conqueror of Earth would be impressive but would draw much attention. I can wear a glove over the others.*

"Which one has the most maneuverability?"

"Minus the black one, they're all about the same." Gavin picked up the silver arm. "This one would be the easiest to install the plasma coil."

"I guess I'll go with that." The silver clasp connecting her prosthesis snapped open and she was once again separated from her left arm.

Chapter 6- Fear of the Past

Drifting through space was a gigantic alien mothership consisting of a gigantic V-shaped wing with a diamond shaped bow, which had two horn-like objects extending from either side of it.

Housed within the ship were the 545 former students taken from a generational ship less than a year ago. Those few considered adults before they were abducted, now acted as leaders of their group.

"I can't believe it's been a year since they disappeared." An attractive youthful Asian woman sat across from a blonde woman of of similar age, who held an infant in her arms.

"Do you think that it's really true? That Denise killed herself and Karl fled in madness?" asked the blonde woman, Brittany Madison. The two of them sat on cushions around a small container used as a makeshift table.

"Why are we talking about them?"

"And Justin and Jacob were lost heroically trying to stop him?" Yuki Amato had been suspicious of the stories from the beginning. "It's true Karl wasn't himself after we lost the *Nomad*, but I couldn't believe that either he or his sister killed themselves. Also an insane person wouldn't have been able to sneak out and pilot a ship before anyone noticed."

"Why not?"

"Well, in the beginning they were saying it was all just an accident when Denise was ejected from the ship." The young mother put the baby down. "You think Karl charged in to save her?"

"It would make sense with him."

"What a hero!"

Yuki scrolled through the pictures of them as students on her handheld. "His mind was mostly in the past where one's relatives were more valuable than one's peers and coworkers. He often spoke of those knights of the second millennium who roamed the Ancient West with their swords and guns who have inspired him."

"That would explain the Sabers' disappearances, but not-"

Alarms rang out throughout the ship interrupting Brittany.

"Attention all students! Koal mothership has been detected!" came over the intercom. "Repeat, Koal mothership has been detected!

All combat personnel to battle-stations! All civilians evacuate to interhull! Repeat, all combat personnel to battle-stations, all civilians evacuate to interhull."

Yuki strapped a pistol to her belt and the two girls waved good-bye before going their separate ways. As Yuki made her way down the dark corridor lit by dim triangular blue lights she met up with a blonde man with blue eyes accompanied by a dark haired man.

"John," she called out to the dark haired boy.

"Where’s my wife and baby?"

"Brittany and your baby are on their way to the shelter."

"Thanks." John felt a little relief.

"It won't matter if we are destroyed here," said Travis Bowie Crockett.

The two stepped on the bridge. On the holographic display in front of them was the image of another ship with the same structure as their own.

"It appears to be another Koal mothership!" yelled John.

"They found us!" exclaimed Travis.

The stolen mothership crewed by the displaced students was soon overtaken by a fully armed ship of the same class.

"The aliens have returned." John looked at the image of the ship in horror.

The students stared at one another in terror.

Chapter 7- Arrival at Tau Ceti

The *Nemesis* arrived on the edge of the Tau Ceti system. On low power, the ship entered orbit around an asteroid. A series of anchoring cables fired from the frigate and the ship slowly pulled towards the asteroid. The ship disappeared behind a holographic field resembling the rocky terrain of the object.

"Well, we're here." Karl rose from his chair.

A figure clad in black armor appeared on the screen with an obsidian long coat over the upper body.

"It is good to see you, Captain," A woman's voice came from behind her obsidian black helmet, with a red eye slit. "The *Starlight* awaits you arrival."

"Shame we can't just take this ship." Karl spun his chair with his right hand as he walked towards Sophia.

"Sadly, a recovered Neith frigate would attract too much attention," Sophia replied.

"Until your faction is back in power, this is still a stolen starship." Lightening hopped up on the captain's chair, which slowly made its final twirl.

Ignoring the cat's statement, the crews of both the *Starlight* and *Nemesis* assembled in the small hanger section of the *Nemesis*.

The skeleton crew manning the *Starlight* included a pair of dark skinned humans from the moons of Jupiter.

Henry, a well-built man dressed in a three-piece suit, and Alice, a slender woman in her midteens wearing a jumpsuit, were joined by the other two remaining members of the crew, Zrela, a well-endowed young Lecaran woman with metallic copper hair and gold eyes, and Reginia, a Koal woman. The latter, like the rest of her race, was completely encased in a refrigerated powersuit covered by a black long coat with gold buckles.

"So what's the plan?" Henry looked up from his pocket computer.

"We need funds and a crew." Karl looked over his crewmen in that section of the vessel. "And we don't have a ship battle-ready for raids."

"What about that frigate?" Henry snuck another look at his

handheld.

"The *Nemesis*," Karl added.

"A Neith warship!" Sophia's eyes widened. "You don't think that would stand out?"

"Well, Black Beard's *Queen Anne's Revenge* was a frigate," Karl recalled. "And Bartholomew Roberts captured a Man o' War."

"And they were both killed in battle." The cat cleaned his tail. "You picked some good role models."

"Who?" Gavin scratched his head.

"They were ancient pirates," Karl commented. "From the-"

"Anyway we'll be using that casino," Sophia interrupted. "I need a few volunteers to remain aboard the *Nemesis*."

Most of the pirates remained silent, not wanting to miss out on drinks and games of chance.

"Shoot." Gavin looked down at his handheld device.

"What's the problem?" Karl worried that something had gone wrong with this ship, or with the repairs on Sophia's arm. "How serious is it?"

"Oh, it's my fantasy elbowball team," Gavin complained, as Jacob moved in to look at Gavin's holoscreen. "My star player isn't scoring any points, and my bench players are scoring all the points."

"I know." Justin looked up from his own handheld computer. "I lost 20,000 Cronos already."

"My team's doing all right," Alice added. "Do you remember what Karl was talking about?"

"Not really." Gavin looked around only to realize that the four of them were the only ones there.

The other pirates already left for the planet while they were absorbed in their game.

An oblong cargo ship with four engines mounted at her stern left the asteroid and made her way to the terraformed world orbiting Tau Ceti. The *Starlight* was not yet suited for piracy as she carried little more than the legal defensive armaments allowed by most star systems. However, the *Starlight* would make the ideal transport and fencing of the pirated goods once they resumed their piracy.

Descending through the atmosphere of the Earth-like planet,

they docked with a spaceport in low orbit connected to an elevator leading down to the planet below.

Having changed on the ship, Karl was now wearing a cape and a fedora with a suit. Sophia wore an oriental dress with a fur-lined cape. Reginia was still in her black armor. Zrela was dressed in a silvery halter top with pair of Terran woman's pants, something which was considered unladylike among the Lecarans.

"So it's actually cheaper for us to dock the ship here than using the one on the actual planet." Karl and the rest of the pirate crew crammed into the small elevator car leading to surface. "I guess that makes sense. But if it cheaper to dock in space, why would anyone use a land-based spaceport?"

"This port charges based upon usage of the elevator and cargo it carries," Reginia explained. "While a land-based charges based upon time spent in the port. So like everything else concerning humanoids, it's ruled by economics."

"And sadly if we didn't have our convenient servants, the feline world would revolve around the cat food exchange." Lightening jumped onto Karl's shoulder. "Also, you might want to do something about the princess."

Karl turned to see Sophia just standing there staring nervously at the crowded elevator.

"What's the matter?"

"Nothing," she replied slowly backing away. "I'll just get the next one."

"That'll double our elevator fee." Reginia grabbed Sophia's wrist with her black gauntlet and dragging the Lecaran girl into the elevator beside Karl. Sophia closed her eyes and began breathing deeply.

The elevator car, now packed like a can of sardines, linked up with half a dozen other cars of the same type before descending several miles down towards the surface.

The elevator train entered a two mile high structure surrounded by hundreds of skyscrapers connected together by a spiderweb-like network of interconnecting bridges.

"This looks different from the last time I was here." Karl looked out the large windows at the city.

"Our contacts have moved to a different city from the last location," Reginia informed him.

"Sadly, not all parts of a planet are the same." Lightening's eyes followed a flock of birds.

Karl glanced down at Sophia who still had her eyes closed but had stopped breathing heavily. He waited for her to respond, but she gave no reaction.

"Sophia?" The doors slid open and she slipped down as the crew exited the cramped space. "Are you all right?"

Karl dragged Sophia out of the elevator and leaned her against the wall. She slowly opened her ruby red eyes.

"Don't freeze me again!" escaped her dark yellow lips. Sophia suddenly blinked and seemed to regain her composure. She took a deep breath and stood up on her own.

"What happened?" Karl had never seen her act like this before.

"I'm fine." Sophia placed her hand on her chest and took a deep breath. "I just need some air."

She's never had an issue with elevators before, Karl thought as they made their way through the starport lobby. *Is this a delayed reaction to the memory restoration drug the Neith agent forced on her?*

Karl frowned with worry, staying close to her as they made their way to the casino.

Chapter 8- The Collector Prince

Orbiting a red dwarf star was a former planet of the Neith Empire now calling itself the Principality of Talon.

A knock came from beyond a set of double doors leading into a stone bath chamber.

"Your Highness. The report from Luna has arrived."

"Enter." Prince Ulai rolled his reddish purple eyes towards the door while his metallic copper hair was washed by a young maid, her body covered in only a light blue towel.

A soldier entered dressed in the silvery coat of the old Neith Empire.

"The battle for Luna ended in victory, but a fourth of our ships were lost in the battle."

The young soldier stood at attention while two other maids entered the chamber. One carrying a set of towels and the other presenting a uniform.

"I see." Ulai rose from the water and his bath maid dried and dressed him. "Double the fee for the ships that were lost, and of course if they don’t agree to those terms, have our forces pull out immediately. What of this Auction of Worlds?"

"We haven’t found anything else more of noteworthiness, Your Highness," the soldier reported. "The only item of note is that the Titan Prince Alec may be attending."

"I suppose he’ll be looking for some advantage over our forces next time he starts encroaching on my territory." The prince took a drink from a small glass. "Well, I suppose it is time we paid a visit to our red blood neighbor. Ready the second fleet and prepare for battle."

"Not this again," the soldier said under his breath.

In the nearest star system orbiting the yellow star, Aten, was the terriformed world, Osiris. The Duke of Osiris, Prince Alec, scratched his blonde hair as he went of the inventory of his most prized possessions.

"Should I arrange them by color or by material?" He stared intently at the rows of glassware.

On one wall he had arranged the carnival glass by type, going horizontally along the shelf and vertically by colors of the rainbow. But what was he to do about the milkglass pieces that were cast from the same molds as those of the carnival glass? Should he start another wall for every color of milkglass?

"When I started this collection, all I had of the milkglass was the pink and the white. And do I want to have the black carnival glass next to the white milkglass or have them on opposite ends of the rainbow?" Prince Alec turned to a row of clear glassware. "And of course what to do when I have every color of the depression glass. I've mostly been limited to clear, green, and pink. Yet there are so many colors and who knows what I might find at the Auction of Worlds?"

He turned to a butler who stood frozen in fear against the wall. The royal servants lived in terror of the idea of entering the glassware rooms. The prince valued his collection so much that he insisted on handling each piece personally.

"Your Highness, I'm afraid that this is not my area of training. Perhaps one of the maids might be of more assistance."

"No, last time the maids suggested using them for serving guests." Prince Alec pulled a newly arrived orange depression glass tray. "You know these artifacts are thousands of years old. Sometimes I wonder if these younger girls are just random members of the middle class looking for a step up the social ladder." He compared the tray to its carnival glass counterpart. "Perhaps I could use a feminine touch with this though, but my sisters are into men, not glass. Curious. As for my backstabbing cousins, I'd sooner trust them with my life than my property."

"I'm sorry, Your Highness." The butler wiped the sweat from his face. "But I do have to deliver the messages from your father, His Highness, Prince Charlemagne, and your mother, Princess-"

"Okay, go ahead." Prince Alec interrupted.

"Your father's was regarding your lack of progress in selecting a suitor. He wants Her Majesty to see her great-grandchildren before she passes into Heaven."

"Remind him that she's only 106 years old and has plenty of time left."

Alec stepped onto a small lift in order to reach the top shelf.

"Also remind him that Her Majesty was in no rush to even be a grandmother. Also who does Father think I'm going to find out here? Most of the new colonists are married workers bringing their families along."

"Your mother's messages lead into that. She is concerned that proximity to a counter-revolutionary Neith lord's territory may contribute to the lack of colonists and turn the entire venture into a waste of taxpayer money."

"Maybe I should have collected something simpler like ancient computers or combustible transports," Prince Alec mumbled under his breath. "But at least I didn't get into the endless nightmare of fashion dolls or robot action figures. Praise the Lord, I didn't end up like Aunt Grace with her fake fingernail collection." Alec looked down at his butler. "Tell Mother-"

"Your Highness, please forgive the interruption," a woman's voice announced over the castle's communication system. "Ships from Talon have begun gathering on the edge of our space."

"Prepare the fleet." Prince Alec gently placed his glass tray on the shelf and the lift lowered him down to the floor. "I will lead the fleet personally. Have a security team guard the glass chamber. Thieves and vandals are to be shot on sight." Alec turned to his butler. "Tell Mother I'm in the middle of negotiations with Prince Ulai."

Chapter 9- The Return to Venus

A long slender diamond shaped craft with forward-swept wings descended into the yellow-orange clouds of Venus.

"How does it feel returning home?" asked one of the officers.

"We should have been allowed to finish off the rebels." The vehicle carrying the Neith Admiral Dalia jointed a small flotilla of brightly lit atmospheric vessels. "There is nothing greater that returning victorious but returning in defeat and parading as though it were victory is so hollow."

The ship came towards Cralton, which hovered above the crushing toxic atmosphere. Like many of the oldest settlements, it was constructed from some of the original ships that carried their race to the Sol System. The five diamond shaped platforms were connected by bridges to form an even large diamond from which spires had grown. The towers had come to cover the diamond over the centuries.

Having circled the city twice, Dalia's craft came towards a platform attached to one of the central spires.

Is this really necessary?" She walked down the gangplank extending from the ship. *Celebrations should be for victories, not unnecessary retreats.*

She was surrounded by other Federation officers and members of the senate. Jarl Narkren was dressed in a white coat. His metallic gold hair was slicked back and his glove covered hands were placed behind his back. While the other politicians were pleased with her return, the purple eyes of Narkren glared.

"We thank you for your great service to the nation." Narkren picked up a small medal from a wooden box held by his aide. He leaned in and placed the metal around her neck. "Remain in the city until I call upon you."

"Understood." She saluted. *I wish you wouldn't keep wasting my time here.*

She was escorted into one of the government buildings, which had once been a temple. While she was never religious, she failed to see the benefit of new regime's removal of the old gods without an adequate replacement.

Her people had no history of a purely secular society.

However, the Terran's failed experiments indicated that the Neith Federation could not go on without a supreme being for more than a century or two. Even the Terran nations ultimately fell back into monarchy in the blink of an eye after Earth was taken from them.

Narkren seems only concerned with maintaining the present system with no ambition for the future. Perhaps we need someone stronger to lead our people into the future.

As she was led into the next chamber, she noticed the departure of the civilians leaders with the exception of Narkren. Her attending officer was also gone.

The soldiers were dressed in white uniforms with black cuffs indicating they were Narkren's personal operatives.

Narkren turned towards her and each of the soldiers aimed a pistol at her.

"What is the meaning of this?" yelled Admiral Dalia, standing before Jarl Narkren.

"Your actions during your last battle called into question your loyalty." Narkren's men removed the sword at her side. "Ensuring the safety and stability of Venus is far greater than that of any off-world territory. At this time, there is a greater threat to deal with than those mere rebels."

"Have you forgotten my record during the revolution." She felt like strangling the man in front of her. "My actions were in complete service to the Federation, and to allow another breakaway state to form is unacceptable."

"We must consider how many loyalists you killed when you obliterated Von Braun City in that asteroid drop of yours." Narkren did not even try to hide his distaste for Admiral Dalia. "And had you not made that orbital strike, the Lunar forces would likely not have chased down your fleet, resulting in the loss of valuable warships. For the moment the population will see you as a hero while we conduct a classified trial."

So I'll be executed and erased from all official record if I am convicted or be reported a victim of counter-revolutionary assassins if they find me innocent.

The white-coated men led her away to an elevator leading to the lower levels of the city.

Chapter 10- Beach Bounty Hunters

As Karl, Sophia, and their party reached the city, the group from the red ship, *Crimson Blade,* had already taken a detour to one of the beaches of the planet.

Trying to relax, with some members of the group being more skilled at having a good time than others, yielded mixed results.

"This is completely pointless." Ray looked over the holographic screen of his computer. "Why did you have to bring us here? Relaxation is a waste of time. Time is money."

"Recall our sensitivities, please. Allergies. It is necessary for Surge to completely recover from his exposure to the cleaner used on that elevator." B-10 stretched out on the sand in a black bikini with a pair of dark sunglasses over her eyes. "Also, I am not sure all my systems are functioning properly. It's only been a year or so since I was stabbed."

"You just wanted to read those old comics you're projecting into your glasses." The boy could make out the faint comic panels on the lenses.

"They're called Manga," she informed him. "I already ran out of the Ancient America comics a week ago, and you said I should study up on humanity, to better understand them."

"I didn't tell you to become a nerd." Ray viewed the fiction of the past as pointless waste of data. "I meant you should learn by observing organics in environment."

"This is no different from when scholars used to study poems to better understand the society that the writers came from." B-10 was making an argument with her own mechanical logic. "Denise was most helpful in providing preinvasion literature."

"My pleasure," said Denise.

"What does murder in a store specializing in Christmas decoration represent?" This was a reference to a thick book entitled *An Innovative Murder for the Season* by Deborah DR Kralich, which was face up on a table beside her chair.

Ray tossed the murder mystery novel to B-10 who caught it by the spine.

"Humanity's need to push forward and overcome every

obstacle placed before it." She caressed the book lovingly. "One of my favorites."

"And an insurance agent solving crimes?" Ray scoffed.

"That character was assisting the police officer." Denise tried to justify the plot.

"Ridiculous," said Surge. "Only a good bounty hunter can pull that off."

As Ray attempted to come up with an argument over how absurd B-10's statement was, a man walked up to them.

"Hey, baby." The man came on to B-10. "How about ditching the kid and catching a drink?"

"I'm sorry but my son would just be devastated if I left for a second." She gave an emotionless lie as she wrapped her arm around Ray.

Ray just froze in a state of shock.

The young man stepped back.

"I understand," he said with a nervous look on his face. He trembled a little just before he left.

Ray regained his senses, pushing away from B-10.

"What did you do that for!?" the boy demanded, rising to his feet.

"I had no interest in that man and thought I would let him down the easy way."

"And you had to do things that way?" he yelled. "Of all things you could have said, you had to drag me into it. Is there some wrong with…?"

"Kira is dressed," she stated, completely distracting Ray from his rant.

He turned around to see Kira, dressed in a one-piece bathing suit with a frilly skirt to cover the base of her white tail.

"Let’s see if you can handle me when I’m not at a hundred percent," Surge smirked, expecting Denise to pick up his challenge.

Denise was wearing a red bikini.

This did not deter her from accepting his challenge.

Surge was carrying three wooden swords.

"If you're going to come with us on missions," Surge handed Denise two swords and stepped back, "you'll need to train more with your weapons."

Denise came at him, swinging her swords.

He stepped out of the way and extended his bokuto in the path of her ankle, causing her to trip face forward into the sand.

"You lose." Surge pointed his sword at her.

"That was dirty." Denise stood back up and raised her practice weapons again.

"Criminals don't play nice." The bounty hunter rested his wooden sword on his shoulder. "Remember your encounter with the slavers and your brother's pirates."

"All right, all right."

"Time for a break." Surge walked over to his beach chair.

A waitress in a blue bikini brought a tray with grilled fish and a banana split, condiments on the side. Surge took the fish and dumped it on the ice cream before topping it with mustard, relish, almonds, sliced bell pepper, cottage cheese, and finally bacon bits. Surge took his spoon and chopped up the soft fish and the banana, before proceeding to stir everything together.

Denise and Ray watched in horror as Surge placed the spoonful of his concoction into his mouth.

"I don't see why did Denise is bothered, she eats chocolate and peanut butter together," Kira opined before taking off and running into the water.

"Hey, people have eaten chocolate and peanut butter candy for centuries." Denise had never lived in a world where chocolate and peanut butter were not available together.

"I've heard rumors that ancient humans ate them together, but peanut butter became rare after the fall of Earth." Ray looked on with disappointment at Surge and Denise. "I guess most people developed sense enough to stop ruining their chocolate when peanuts were reintroduced to commoners like us."

"That is delicious." Surge was about to take another bite of his fish sundae but turned towards Denise and Ray. "Do you guys want some?"

Denise picked up her wooden sword, ready to strike the male bounty hunter.

Chapter 11- The Masters' Rendezvous

On the same planet as Karl Sabers and his colleagues, yet in a different location, looking out over the city of Xehelken was a tall man in his late twenties.

His left hand rested on the grip of his basket-hilt broadsword extending from under a black velvet coat and his right held a glass of orange liquor.

He sipped the liquor with understated relish.

"Master Charles," called the voice of a young woman. "Ashley Claymore has arrived. Along with his, um, assistant, as he describes her."

Charles Sanwell turned towards a beautiful young woman with pale blue skin and raven black hair.

He felt a rush of pleasure at the sight of his servant although he was not pleased with her news.

"Thank you, Selina." Charles put his drink down. "Show them in."

A blonde woman with gray wolf-like ears and a fluffy tail was followed by an old man with a white mustache and a dragon-head cane in his gloved left hand. Both were dressed in matching three-piece suits with frock coats.

"I see you're still keeping your Antarctican slaves around." The old man looked over Selina. "You'd be better off selling these hybrid clones and buying some androids."

"In my mind they are employees, not slaves," Charles stated. "Each of them has a name and is free to leave if they chose to."

"Why did you call me here? I thought you didn't want us seeing each other until the Auction?"

"I'm not happy to see you. Don't get that idea. It was necessary."

"Why?"

"It concerns those children from that Koal vessel and our royal heir." Sanwell took a drink. "It's possible that advertising the lost colonist may attract Blood Terra. I thought the royal guest is attracting attention of the Neith as well? A star navy we might be able handle, but terrorists are another matter."

"I wouldn't be concerned with that, my friend." Ashley glanced at his servant. "Trust in the Barley."

Isabella gave him a perky smile.

"Do you allow such insolence from your servants?"

"I don't let anything slaves do bother me as long as they do their work and obey orders."

"I prefer my servants to give me pleasure."

"Emotional or physical pleasures?"

"Both." Sanwell finished his drink and glanced at his beautiful servant. "She keeps me warm at night when it is cold. Her name is Selina and I bought her at an auction similar to the one we are planning right now."

"I failed to see how she keeps you warm when she came from the coldest place that humans can even attempt to inhabit."

As their masters began speaking of them as if they were not there, the two female slaves began watching each other instead of the dominators.

Selina went to a desk, opened a drawer, and pulled out a bag of soft jelly candy. She walked toward the males and offered each one a sample of the treat.

They both declined.

However, this action halted their conversation and their eyes followed her as she went to Isabella and shared the confection with the tall blonde Lrakian.

Nonplussed for a moment, the two masters watched their slaves as they ate.

"Now, as I was saying, Claymore-"

Simultaneously both males turned their backs on the females and forgot they were even in the room.

"- I think our best course of action is…"

Chapter 12- The Selection

A group of humanoids with pale blue skin advanced forward. Each was dressed in a black uniform trimmed in gold. They descended into the lower section of a warehouse with a village of prefabricated structures housed within.

The students from the *Nomad* peered out at their new captors with interest.

There they saw two Terrans standing on a platform overlooking the enclosed compound, an old man with a dragon cane and a young man with a sword.

"Who are they?" John looked at the first humans he had seen besides his fellow students.

"I don't know." Travis pulled one of the mechanical guns left over from the *Nomand's* museum section.

"Do you think they are here to rescue us?"

"If they're working with the Koal, they are either captors or collaborators."

"But we don't know if these blue people are the Koal. We never got a chance to look inside the suits."

"They were in a Koal ship."

"But when we damaged the suits there was cold air coming out of them."

Accompanied by their Koal associates each man looked into the living quarters of the students.

"Greetings lost children of Earth, your current plight is at an end." Sanwell's voice broadcast throughout the chamber. "I am Charles Sanwell and I apologize for the current living conditions that you are forced to endure, but it is a necessary inconvenience as you are a people without a nation. However, through our Auction of Worlds you will be adopted into the one of the galactic star kingdoms as a lost tribe of Earth."

Sanwell stepped back and Claymore stood before them.

"You safety will require the most eligible maidens among you to volunteer their service." The blue aliens dragged many of the girls from their chambers. "You will, of course, be required to undergo a physical examination."

"I was hoping we'd be done with physical examinations once our school lives were over." Brittany watched as Selina and Isabella approached.

"Why does that one have a tail?" Travis took in the sight of the two alien women.

Selina stepped into their room and looked over both Yuki and Brittany. A series of symbols flashed across the blue skinned alien's monocle.

"This one's pure." Selina removed her monocle and pointed to Yuki.

Travis and John could only watch as Yuki was dragged from the living quarters.

They had no idea what fate would befall her.

Chapter 13- King Bob

The group led by Karl and Sophia arrived at the casino. Floating behind the group was the Oracle, with Lightening perched on top of it.

"So do you think we'll make enough here?" Zrela looked around ready to try her luck.

"Well, we have both these two wonderful artificial intelligences." Karl looked down as the projection of Miss Holo from his handheld. "I'm sure they'll be willing to help out."

"I'm not sure this is the correct course of action." The Oracle scanned the gambling tables. "One might see this as harming organic lifeforms."

"I would have to say that I'm with the Oracle on this." Miss Holo backed up her fellow AI. "I also cannot approve of my students taking part in such an activity as gambling."

"Well, do you have any other ideas?"

"In the past, the casino head would select certain members of the crew to act as dealers, referees, or opponents if needed," Reginia informed succinctly.

A young fair skinned Lrakian woman with short white hair and cat-like ears was approaching. She was dressed in a black harem outfit with a pair of heeled sandals. Unlike Kira, this Lrakian's nails had been sharpened to resemble claws on what was otherwise human hands.

"Captain Sabers," the woman introduced herself. "I am Shiroko, third wife of Pride King Bob. My husband wishes to speak to you."

"Who?" Karl tried his best not to stare at her clothing.

"He's recently acquired the rights to this establishment," she answered.

Shiroko led them beyond the gambling tables.

They walked into a large room with an arena in the middle surrounded by several rows of seats. In his own personal box seat was a male Lrakian with gray catlike ears. Karl, for a split second, could have mistaken King Bob's ears for horns.

At the male Lrakian's side was another black haired Lrakian

woman in a white harem outfit.

"I, Mel, challenge King Bob for right of pride king." A young man with tapered ears and a long catlike tail stepped onto the platform.

Mel drew a black katana.

"Challenge accepted." The short-tailed Lrakian king stepped out of his box into the arena.

King Bob's wives slid a pair gauntlets onto each of his arms. The armor had swords extending from the knuckles onto each arm.

The two alien men wore fur-lined kilts instead of the pants worn by their female counterparts.

Mel charged, swinging his katana at his opponent. King Bob deflected the weapon with right pata before slashing with his left.

Mel jumped back, evading the strike before countering with an upwards swing of his weapon.

King Bob blocked the strike, and as Mel's blade slid along the gauntlet sword, the lower half of Bob's left sword sprang open into three blades, functioning like a trident. Catching Mel's Katana between those blades, Bob executed a simple twist of his arm. The katana snapped in half.

Then King Bob stabbed his challenger in the stomach with the pata on his right arm.

With his challenger vanquished, the pride king returned to his seat. Two of King Bob's wives approached the ring and removed the fallen Lrakian's body.

"So you're the young pirate who picked a fight with the Evlon Temple." King Bob wiped the white alien blood from his weapon before turning his gaze towards Karl. "I have to say I was expecting something more impressive, but I guess you are just a human."

"True he may only be human but he does have certain uses." Lightening stood proudly on Karl's shoulders. "Such as being able to open a can of cat food. And Karl also happens to have excellent petting skills."

"What a strange creature." King Bob looked down at the cat.

"This coming from the kilt-wearing man with cat ears," Lightening commented. "Also, as it appears that you are descended from cats, you should worship me as your greatest ancestor. Now I shall be expecting daily offerings of tuna."

"Captain Sabers." The Lrakian turned his attention from the feline. "I assume that you were looking for a financial backer at this Auction of Worlds."

"How did you know that?"

"It's been a while, Captain Sabers," said a familiar voice. "I trust you've been taking care of my niece."

Karl turned to see a man with long metallic silver hair and ruby red eyes like those of Sophia. Baldassara wore a long white coat with the hilt of a scimitar poking out from his left side. To his right was Nara, whose body was mostly hidden by a purple cloak covering all but the lower half of her face and a few locks of silvery Lecaran hair.

"It's good to see you." Sophia curtsied upon seeing the man.

"Like yourself I have a business arrangement with Lord Baldassara." King Bob rubbed his hands together. "Now that my little duel is over we can get to business."

King Bob led them to his box positioned in front of the arena.

"One of my contacts recently came across a shop which may have acted as a front during your time in storage," Baldassara explained. "There is a small chance they might have some information regarding your sister's whereabouts. There is also an item of value I would like you to acquire for me."

"Why do you need us to get it?" Karl figured that it would have made more sense to send one of Baldassara's other pirates to retrieve what he needed.

"Because the store's owner does not serve Non-Terrans." Baldassara transmitted the directions to Karl and Sophia's handhelds.

"So they'll allow me to shop there. But not the space princess." The feline swatted at a small glowing moth with his paw.

Chapter 14- An Unwanted Reunion

"You two should have worn dresses." Kira looked on with displeasure at Denise and B-10's pantsuits.

"I'm not going to be your dress-up doll again," Denise asserted. "At least I'm dressed for the occasion."

Surge was attired in his faded coat with his katana attached to his belt.

"You know we were supposed to meet with Denise's brother a long time ago." Ray entered the casino directly behind the girls.

"In a place of gambling and drinking. I'm sure those pirates are still here." Surge looked around for any kind of dessert or meat bar.

Reginia approached Surge's group.

"If you're looking for Sophia and the captain, they left a few hours ago."

"What?" Denise staggered back remembering the time a Koal slaver had nearly choked her to death.

"They're running a little errand for me," said King Bob.

"For us," Baldassara corrected.

The Lrakian pride king and Baldassara's allies from the Syndicate looked at each other.

The Lrakian man immediately took notice of Kira.

Kira raised her fist to defend herself. Surge casually placed his left hand just under the guard of his katana.

Ray positioned himself between Kira and B-10.

Denise looked at her comrades, unsure what was happening.

"So the pride defector dressed as a man and acting alone as a bounty hunter." Bob focused directly on Kira, ignoring the humans and the gynoid. "How quaint. When will you outgrow your rebellious stage and take your place as one of my wives?"

"She's a member of my crew." Surge's Japanese sword left its scabbard.

"Now let's be civil about this." Baldassara stepped in front of Bob. "There is no use for us to behave like barbarians."

"Very well, follow me to the arena." Bob smirked at the bounty hunters.

The crew of the *Crimson Blade* was escorted to the dueling

chamber.

Surge stepped into the arena. He drew his sword, waiting for the pride king to step forward.

Baldassara drew his glass scimitar from its sheath.

"I've always wanted a chance to go after that bounty on your head." Surge smiled. "I came close to capturing the Syndicate pirate almost a year ago but unfortunately was forced to settle for a criminal of lesser value."

"Now I remember you, the bounty hunter who collected that annoying cyborg, Thorn." The blade of Baldassara's sword glowed purple. "I suppose I should thank you."

"Yeah and he should've killed that-" Denise cut herself off.

"The amount of money that I'm going to make off you will be thanks enough."

Surge's katana turned blue and the two swords made contact simultaneously. Baldassara angled the sword downward, causing the bounty hunter's sword to slide against the glass blade. Readjusting his wrists, Baldassara re-angled his blade towards Surge's neck.

The bounty hunter's sword stopped the scimitar seconds before it could decapitate the halfbreed. Surge kneed Baldassara in the side. Baldassara stuck Surge's brow with the pommel of his weapon and the bounty hunter collapsed, his Terran blood flowing from the wound.

Baldassara kicked the unconscious Surge onto his back before sheathing his scimitar.

"With blood drawn and my opponent unable to fight, I consider the matter settled."

Nara approached Baldassara as he stepped out of the ring.

"Why did you not finish him off, My Lord?" asked the hooded woman.

"For the moment, he has an alliance with my niece. And he may prove useful in eliminating some of the more useless members of the Syndicate." He handed his sword to Nara. "Like yourself, he could be the offspring of some noble and his slave. I want you to use his genetic material to track down anyone of value."

Chapter 15- The Chase

Sophia and Karl walked with Lightening riding on Karl's shoulder over to a taxi. The vehicle was yellow and black, and looked like an egg on its side, with two parallel rods on each side of it.

They got in the taxi and headed off to the shop called Twin Head's Rare Items, where they were to pick up the item Baldassara was requesting.

Karl figured it was worth going there so long as he and Lightening were careful this time. The taxi drove along the transparent road until it reached the shop. Twin Head's, like all the other shops on the towers, had its entrance on the outside of the building.

The two humanoids walked inside the shop, reacting to the shelves filled with rather bizarre looking objects. Some of the items were organs and body parts in glass jars, others included machine parts that could have come right out of any alien or Terran ships.

"We don't serve your kind here!" yelled the old woman at the desk.

"I am simply accompanying my master." Sophia held up her right hand displaying the slave bracelet on her right wrist.

"If it's a slave, I'll let her in," the shopkeeper relented. "But she must remain with you at all times."

"I feel like snapping her neck." Sophia flexed the synthetic fingers of her left hand, as they moved further into the shop.

Unconcerned, Karl was eyeing an ancient .32 automatic pistol among the machine parts. And there was a box filled with at least fifty rounds of ammunition.

"Karl, do you think the stuff in these jars is eatable." Lightening saw each jar as part of a sealed buffet.

"The word is edible. And, Lightening, you just ate." Karl watched his cat, hoping that he wouldn’t break anything open.

Lightening hoisted his tail and turned his behind to Karl.

As Karl picked up the box and the pistol, he noticed a container similar to the one he had seen in the cargohold of the *Starlight.*

Tucked away in a corner, it had junk piled on top.

He walked over to the container, and saw a price tag of 21,000 Martian credits on it.

"Now this is familiar," Lightening rubbed himself against the casket. "You need to be careful and not wake this one up unless you want to end up buying a harem of space girls."

"So that's what we're here for, right?" Karl pulled out his handheld computer. The image of a container projected from the center of his device.

He turned towards Sophia, who stood starring at the casket-like container in front of her with a look of panic on her face.

"Sophia?"

Sophia immediately ran out the door. Karl put down the merchandise and followed her.

Karl discovered her standing outside with both hands on the railing.

"What happened?"

"When I look at that slave container I see a child with one arm staring back as air around me freezes and the dark surrounds me." Sophia's left hand crushed the metal railing. "Ever since you brought me back from that Federation outpost, I haven't been able to forget the fear of being locked away like that."

"That's not going to happen again." Karl placed his hands on her shoulders. "If anyone does capture you, I'll rescue you just like last time."

"I'm not totally helpless." The wire around her left wrist uncoiled and ignited into a plasma blade.

She deactivated her weapon and leaned in closer to him. Karl put his arms around her. Without warning, she pressed her yellow lips against his. The two of them backed away slowly, their faces red and yellow with blush.

"I would suggest getting a room. But at this point she might faint again," Lightening commented.

Karl returned to the shop while Sophia remained outside trying to regain her composure.

He walked back towards the container.

"You want to see inside?" asked the old woman.

Karl turned around to a shopkeeper woman standing behind

him.

She removed the dust covered junk, then ran her hand along the side until she touched the green panel.

The panel turned blue and the lid became transparent.

He half expected to see a beautiful alien girl in her late teens with strange hair, dressed in a silver gown inside the container.

Instead there was a young Lrakian man with a yellow orange cat-like tail. Embedded in his right wrist was a gold bracelet like Sophia's.

"You're disappointed that it's not a girl?" Lightening smirked.

Thank God, Sophia's bracelet is now deactivated, thought Karl.

Similarly to King Bob, this alien wore a kilt.

I guess all Lrakian men wear kilts, Karl concluded. *King Bob's wives wore pants, and so did Claymore's Lrakian servant.*

"Karl, not sure I like that there is a race of skirt-wearing cat-people." Lightening licked his fur. "You need to rectify the situation of there being more of these cat-eared people than actual cats. Karl, I want kittens."

"So how much for this one?" Karl ignored the feline.

"90,000." The older woman was still staring at the container.

"That's over four times as much as you paid for the princess," Lightening recalled.

And one and a half times what I made on the Starlight.

The man's eyes snapped open and he turned his head towards Karl. The gold irises stared at Karl. The Lrakian placed his hand against the transparent lid of the container.

"Is he supposed to be able to do that?" Karl backed away slowly.

"Lrakians are a rather hardy race." The old shopkeeper was unimpressed. "They were engineered as to be warriors. It's not surprising that he might wake up. Good news is that he should be able carry that container of his."

"I guess, ring him up." Karl still did not feel comfortable with the issue of legal slavery despite this alien being the second one he had bought. He looked down at his handheld and saw the projection of the other item that he had been instructed to purchase.

Karl heard a noise from a weapon's rack. He picked a strangely ornate looking carbine.

Looking into the scope, he saw what appeared to be a family group of well-dressed Lecarans. The family had ten members with eight children of varying ages, each having ruby red eyes.

A hail of orange plasma bolts was fired at the Lecarans.

Karl quickly moved the scope away from his eye.

He was not sure about the identity of the alien in the recording, but if Baldassara wanted it, the rifle was likely one of the weapons used to execute Sophia's family.

He wondered what purpose Baldassara had for wanting something like this.

He believed it could perhaps lead to Sophia's sister.

Deciding to buy the guns, Karl walked over to a deck with a hologram monitor and keyboard. Beside the keyboard was a hole designed to transfer money from a buyer's funds to the seller’s account. Karl pulled out his new handheld computer and placed it in the hole. The number 200,000 appeared above the computer, then dropped down to 89,000. The woman handed Karl a slave control rod, which was gold and looked about like a flashlight. Instead of a glass lens and a light bulb, it had a blue gem about the size of a thumbnail.

"Karl?" Lightening yawned. "When do we eat?"

"That's a good question." Karl picked up a gray container filled with the ammo for his new gun.

He pulled out the .32, loaded it, and placed it in his jacket pocket. He would have preferred a larger caliber gun, but the .32 would make a fine addition to his collection of ancient mechanical firearms.

Karl stepped outside, carrying the carbine wrapped in cloth.

"So is this the package?" Sophia looked over the Lrakian following behind Karl.

"That's what we were told to get." Karl hoped that she would not ask to look at the carbine.

"Not sure what good a Lrakian is except as muscle." Sophia turned back to the taxi.

"So what's a Lecaran good for other than a secondary source of money after the Terrans?"

The Lrakian swung his tail back and forth like a cat.

"Slave with a tongue." Sophia glared over her shoulder.

"And not too long ago we picked up a slave with a mouth." Lightening looked up at Sophia.

The three got into the taxi, speeding back towards the building housing the casino. Without warning, blasts of plasma started firing behind them.

"Auto pilot offline," relayed a voice from the taxi's computer.

"What now?"

"Can you fly this thing?" Karl's eyes darted between Sophia and their new companion.

Sophia grabbed the joystick and took control of the craft, as a trio of small slender fighters appeared behind them.

"We should drop to a lower altitude," Miss Holo called from Karl's handheld. "If we keep this up innocent people could get hurt."

Karl unwrapped the carbine and smashed the back window of the taxi before opening fire on their pursuers. A gold shot from the carbine penetrated the cockpit of a fighter.

As Sophia continued to dodge the enemy fire, a blast hit the taxi's right engine pod. The taxi took a nosedive, and three smaller craft followed behind. The Lrakian man jerked the sword from Karl's scabbard.

Before Karl had a chance to react, the side hatch of the taxi flew open. The cat-eared man jumped on top of one the enemy craft and slashed open the cockpit.

He ripped the pilot from his seat and threw him off.

"AHHH!!!" The man fell to the ground of the planet.

The Lrakian opened fire at the remaining fighter. The last of the attacking fighters exploded behind them.

Sophia pulled back on the joystick in attempt to level the taxi. The entire vehicle jolted. Karl looked down to see the Lrakian controlled fighter pushing up the taxi.

"Captain Sabers, I am detecting similar craft on approach to this section," the disembodied voice of Miss Holo reported.

"Well, that's not good."

The damaged vehicle descended into the lower levels of the city.

Chapter 16- Deal Breaker

Karl and Sophia made their way into a Gothic structure with a gigantic spire and brightly colored stain glass windows. While there were small churches and chapels aboard the *Nomad*, they were nothing this grand. This was almost medieval and even had the stages of the Crucifixion.

"So this is what one of the cathedrals of the Martian Church looked like." Sophia's glass heels echoed down the aisle. She seemed even more amazed at the place than Karl.

Karl remembered some of the older photos from his Earthborn ancestors and the white gowns worn by the brides in the cathedrals. Then the image of Sophia in a white dress entered his mind.

"They didn't have any of these left on Earth after you invaded?" Karl hoped that not all the historic structures of Earth had been lost.

"The imperial court feared we might be corrupted by an Earthling religion." She slowly scanned over each piece of stained glass. "While I'm sure some churches survived our rule on Earth, Venus was completely void of any Terran sects."

"I guess the church would be the oldest institution to survive the Fall of Earth," Karl commented.

"Over three and half thousand years since our Lord Jesus Christ ordained Saint Peter as the first Pope," said a voice from behind. They turned to see a young Lecaran man dressed in black robes with white collar and a silver crosses hanging from his neck. "Greetings, I am Father Gabriel and welcome to St. Ignatius. If you're planning on attending the evening Mass, you're still a half hour early."

The Church is accepting aliens now. Karl noticed that the deep red eyed young man in front of him did not have the gold or silver hair of a Lecaran but the blonde hair of a Terran. *Another halfbreed, I guess. This makes three now.*

"I'm sorry. We were just having a look around."

"Actually, we'll stick around for it," Sophia decided.

"What?" Karl looked at her in surprise.

Sophia dragged his head closer to hers.

"Look, this'll be a good place to hide out for an hour or so until the coast is clear," she whispered.

"All right." *How does this go again? Greet each other, sing a few hymns, take a nap, then go eat.*

"However, I must let you know, in the event your slave chooses to seek holy orders, under intergalactic law you will have to relinquish ownership."

They looked to see the Lrakian standing behind them.

"I will have to discuss my intended purpose with my new masters before making such as choice." The Lrakian glanced at Karl and Sophia.

"You have a name?" Father Gabriel shook hands with the slave.

"Tut."

So the cat-eared alien is named after a pharaoh and cost me more than Sophia, Karl thought. *This whole trip is going to be a waste of time and money if he stays here.*

The three humanoids took their places in the pews. Karl picked up the Missilette in hopes of finding out how to proceed. The small book mostly seemed to list different apps to be downloaded and used in conjunction with the saint of the day's feast.

Perhaps this could be used as a code for his pirate crew.

"The grace of our Lord Jesus Christ, and the love of God, and the communion of the Holy Spirit be with you all."

"And also with you," the congregation said in unison.

"Please load in app 215 and the corresponding Bible verse for the reading of the Word."

Karl loaded the app and tried to follow along but his eyes became heavy.

"-Lord be with you."

Karl opened his eyes not knowing how much time had passed.

"May almighty God bless you," Father Gabriel continued. "The Father, and the Son, and the Holy Spirit. Go in peace, glorifying the Lord by your life."

After Mass ended, Karl returned to the enemy craft sitting outside the church.

Who were these guys?

They were undisturbed during the Mass that Karl had slept

through. He assumed their attackers were gone or had been dealt with.

"Miss Holo." Karl activated his handheld. "Can you access any data on this ship and why we were attacked?"

"Just a moment." Miss Holo deftly hacked the craft's data recorder.

"Are you sure that's them?" asked the first recorded voice.

"A Neith and Lrakian led by a man with a curved sword," the other man's voice recounted. "They have to be the bounty hunters."

"Once we deal with them, our brother, Thorn, will be avenged and we will report back to Master Greenbreath."

The recording cut off.

"Who's Thorn?" Sophia asked.

"He assaulted Denise once. Surge arrested him." Karl looked back over at the one-man skycraft. "I guess we'll have to call another taxi to get back to the others. Who wants to fly this thing back?"

"You want to keep it?" Sophia was not impressed, and the small craft did not even have a canopy anymore.

"Spoils of war," Karl stated. "After what they put us through, I think we're entitled to one of their skycraft."

Their craft landed on the platform adjacent to the tower housing the casino.

Tut exited the smaller craft and followed Karl and Sophia into the casino where they found at least a dozen female Lrakians surrounding Denise and Surge.

The latter being knocked out on the floor.

"At least it's not you passed out this time." Lightening jumped on Karl's shoulder.

"What's going on here?"

"These bounty hunters were trying to interfere with pride matters." Bob pointed his left weapon at Karl. "It's none of your concern."

"If my sister is going to be surrounded by-" Karl paused.

"My wives." King Bob stepped towards Karl. "The traitor among the bounty hunters was once part of my pride and she must be punished."

Karl placed his left hand on his sword.

"Rest assured should I die outside of a duel, my pride will

hunt you until I am avenged." King Bob endeavored to stare down the pirates.

"If you're going to keep this up, someone from the Syndicate higher ups will have to take care of you." Baldassara stepped between the two groups. "Now I suggest we conclude our business first and you can arrange your duels off world."

Baldassara turned to the Lrakian man. "Should any harm befall the one they call Sophia, we will not only eliminate you but your entire bloodline as well."

Bob took notice of the Lrakian male.

"I see you brought my package." Bob looked over Tut. One of his wives strapped his wrist blade to his left arm.

"What are you doing?"

"This man is a son of one of the pride kings that fell at my hand, and as such his life is forfeit." Bob's right hand weapon was then attached.

"You know by law that this is my right to challenge, not yours," Kira protested.

"I don't like where this is going," Karl said, under his breath.

"Karl, you are still Tut's owner until you hand him over," Lightening whispered.

And we could use more crewmen. Karl tried to come up with justification for not handing over the Lrakian. "Sophia, how long will it take for our new member to pay us back?"

"About half a year, depending on loot acquisition," she answered.

"Seven months, fifteen days, and twenty-three hours," said the Oracle.

"What is that?"

King Bob and his wives turned to the floating disk.

"Behold, I am the emissary of the Elder voice." The Oracle switched to his booming tone.

"I follow Sekhmet, goddess of war, not some made up race of ancient super aliens." King Bob scrapped his blades together.

"Oh!" The Oracle switched back to his normal auto setting.

"Egyptians, let's try this again." Lightening jumped from Karl's shoulder, landing on the Oracle. "Behold I am Lightening, divinely ordained feline ruler of the galaxy."

Wasn't Sekhmet a lioness? Karl's mind wandered slightly.

King Bob gave no reaction but his wives each backed away slowly.

"This is the police. Surrender or be destroyed."

A loud siren followed the voice.

"Three of the aircraft are currently circling this floor," Miss Holo informed anyone interested. "Their weapons are armed."

"Well, boy." Bob glared at Karl. "I'll leave him with you for the moment. We'll have to continue this another time."

Bob's pride dispersed, leaving behind the pirates and bounty hunters.

"I guess we will have to make ourselves scarce as well," said Reginia.

"I would personally prefer to avoid conflict with the local coppers." Baldassara began walking away with Nara following behind. "If you want to avoid meeting with more trouble, come with me."

B-10 slung the still unconscious Surge over her shoulder and they followed the Syndicate pirate.

A few moments later the Tau Ceti forces, dressed in the pale red uniforms of Mars, charged in to discover the casino deserted.

Chapter 17- On the Sky Yacht

Having escaped aboard Baldassara's sky yacht, Karl's and Surge's crews made plans to leave the planet orbiting Tau Ceti.

"Well that was a bust." Sophia tossed her dress over the side of a folding screen in the corner the cabin. "So what are we going to do with the Lrakian?"

"I agree. I haven't had anything to eat this whole trip." Lightening stretched out on the couch beside Karl.

"I guess Tut will be part of the crew until he pays back what we spent on him."

"I'm sure he'll pay you back. Your debt collection won't end in failure like last time." Lightening glanced over at the screen where Sophia was changing.

"Captain Sabers!" Nara's voice called from Karl's handheld. "Lord Baldassara requests your presence along with the second package."

"So what does he want?" Sophia stepped out from behind the screen in a short black dress with long sleeves and a gold chain acting as a belt.

"For her safety, Lord Baldassara requests that Her Highness remain in her cabin."

"I will not!" Sophia snatched the handheld computer from Karl's hand. "Where was this concern when he sent us to pick up the Lrakian?"

"I don't think Tut identifies as the Lrakian." Lightening walked onto Karl's lap.

"The incident during your errand has indicated that new steps need to be taken regarding your protection." Baldassara came on the line. "At the time, I was unaware of my niece's penchant for attracting trouble."

"The absence of my presence will be your punishment until we get off world." Sophia sat down on the bed and turned away from them.

"I sure the absence of your presence will be forgotten as soon as you don't show up." Lightening jumped on Karl's shoulder.

Sophia threw the pocket computer, which sailed by Karl on his way out the door. The door slammed shut behind him.

I hope she didn't break this. Karl picked up his handheld. The device made a strange squeal. *Never heard that before, I'll have to have Gavin look at it.*

He headed down a corridor lined with a pattern of silver roses on his way to the Syndicate lord's quarters. The door slid open into a wood panel cabin with Baldassara seated at his desk.

"So you think that will somehow lead to her sister?" Karl handed the carbine to Baldassara.

"You saw. I trust she knows nothing of this." Baldassara looked down the scope.

"No, since the encounter with Narkren's agent she's been-"

"Been having nightmares," Baldassara predicted. "Whether she remembered her past or not, that drug they gave her would have forced her to relive her past. Unfortunately tracking down one of the royal reprogrammers would be difficult at this point."

"Reprogrammer?"

"Political assassinations were not uncommon." He gently placed the carbine on his desk. "In order to maintain effective heirs, the children who survived such events were often in need of reeducation."

"Like brainwashing?"

"That's a harsh term for it."

"Lightening, you did something for me when the Koal took me from the *Nomad*?" Karl turned toward the tabby.

"Feline hypnotic therapy does not work on the stubborn." Lightening wiped his face. "It works best on the passive, the recently shell-shocked. And prey."

"Gee, thanks." Karl rolled his eyes.

"You're welcome." Lightening jumped down and stretched out on the floor.

"Once you've left Tau Ceti, our best course is to make for the Principality of Talon." Baldassara attempted to transfer the coordinates to Karl's broken handheld, but the data failed to transmit. Baldassara reached in his desk and pulled out a transparent coin and rolled it across the wooden surface towards Karl.

"That'll have the data needed to reach the rendezvous point. The ruler is a former Neith noble. You would do best to arrive in that stolen frigate of yours before those other vessels under your command make their presence known."

"Guess I better go make up with Sophia." Karl slipped the data coin in the pocket of his waistcoat before returning to his cabin.

Remaining in his office after Karl left, Baldassara turned towards a shimmer in the corner. The cloaked figure faded into view.

"Are you sure you want the second princess out of your sight?" Nara opened her cloak walking towards the desk.

"The warlord running that system has a number of former Neith warships that could easily be reclaimed by a legitimate heir. Besides forcing her on the throne is only necessary if her sister is truly dead and all genetic traces of her are purged."

"So growing an heir artificially is still on the table." Nara was seated on the edge of his desk.

"Yes, but it would need to be the child of the first, not second in line for the throne, and while raising a new heir from scratch would make an easier-to-control puppet, we're still looking at half a decade before the child could make an effective figurehead."

Chapter 18- The Unwelcome Mission

When the guards come I could try taking one of their weapons. In the gravity prison, Dalia stared up at the opening of her bronze cell twenty feet above her. *The other inmates could serve as a temporary crew in exchange for a military pardon.*

She was grateful she had at least been allowed the dignity of keeping her uniform, instead of being forced to wear a prison dress.

Dalia heard the sound of footsteps coming. She moved to an oblong block meant to serve as a bed located in the corner of the room. The admiral positioned herself on the block with her feet against the end of the bench, her soles fixed to the wall.

Walking directly across from her were two guards wearing black helmets with visors covering the upper halves of their faces. Following was a Lecaran man. He had metallic silver hair and a blue tinted monocle covering one of his yellow eyes.

With the gravitational pull altered in her cell, it looked to Dalia as though the men were walking along the same wall her boots were pressed against.

He turned and stood parallel to her. At any moment the wall could become the floor and would pull her towards it.

"To allow another breakaway state to form is unacceptable." He pulled a yellow jewel attached to a silver chain out of his pocket. "Wouldn't you agree?"

Dalia's weight suddenly shifted from her back to her feet and she now stood upright, and the bed was now vertical against the wall.

The man came towards her with a smile on his face. Placing his back against the wall beside Dalia's vertical bed, he was trying to forestall falling down when the gravity shifted again.

As soon as a guard flipped a switch, the gravity change pulled them both flat against the floor of the cell.

"I fail to see the why the aristocracy insisted on designing gravity prisons without a physical door to cover them." He stood back up and tossed the gem in his hand straight in the air. The object curved towards the wall before hovering at the gravitational shift point.

"State your name and rank." Dalia stood back up to face him.

"My name is Haman, just a humble political adviser," he answered, bowing to her. "And I've also been following your career very closely, and I know of your interest in rising to the political level."

"How would an agent of the political world benefit from someone like myself? Surely you could find someone more suitable to occupy your time."

"Not at all. We would need a strong hand to guide this nation should Narkren leave us."

"What you're suggesting could be considered treason by some." Dalia slowly circled around Haman. "I'm already under a secret trial and would prefer not to find myself sent straight to the surface camps."

"Narkren is responsible for far greater atrocities then just exiling his enemies to the surface." Haman removed his handheld from his pocket. "But I have good news regarding your trial. It's now to be conducted while you are off world on your temporary assignment."

"So I'll only have a convenient accident if they decide on guilt." Dalia crossed her arms. "And what can I do for our glorious Narkren before he has me erased?"

"Sending an Admiral to take out a princess." the man smirked. "One of our frigates was stolen by a criminal who claims descent from the old royal family. Your fleet will be redeployed to track down the criminal."

"You would send out an entire fleet on an errand to track down one ship!"

"Narkren has become quite obsessed with that." Haman stared at the floating gem caught in the gravitational midpoint. "He even lost one of his personal agents during this little hunt. Of course he claims she is a mere impostor, but for someone who considers the safety and stability of Venus far greater than that of any off world territory, his need to personally defer resources to the hunt for a fake princess off world is certainly suspicious."

"I see your point." Dalia dropped down on the slab and crossed her legs. "So bringing back her head would put me in Narkren's good graces momentarily."

"If nothing else, I would like you to take this invitation to something called the Auction of Worlds." Haman walked closer to Dalia. "Narkren saw no point to dispute the fact that one of the items they are offering is the hand of a princess."

"I would agree with not being so quick to disregard this possible opportunity." She smiled, unfastening the top of her uniform. "We wouldn't want either the Titan Empire or the Mars Imperium to gain another advantage over us. I shall attend this Auction of Worlds and see what can be gained from it."

Just outside the cell a fully armored man stood guard making sure that the discussion and activities of Admiral Dalia and Haman remained undisturbed.

Chapter 19- A Ship in Distress

"Damn it." Surge sat down in his chair aboard the *Crimson Blade*. "We were so close to capturing Baldassara. And none of you tried to wake me while we were surrounded by all those bounties?"

"You would have been useless even if you were awake," B-10 stated.

"We were outnumbered, and with your head injury, capturing him would have been impossible." Kira stretched her arms. "The weaker races like yourselves I can handle, but I haven't fought another Lrakian since my childhood."

Kira walked down the hall leaving the three of them.

"I was able to determine that both Marth Greenbreath and Baldassara will be attending the auction." Ray smirked. "I had to hack the network on Baldassara's skyyacht."

"Surge, we're detecting a nearby distress signal," B-10 announced over the communication system, despite most of the crew being on the bridge.

"Do we have to?" Surge groaned as he stood up.

"Denise would say, 'God wants us to help those in need'." Ray glanced over at Surge. "It's close to dinner time. Do you really want to be on her bad side for more than just your eating habits?"

"They appear to be under attack."

"I guess we could make a few extra bucks off a couple pirates." Surge made his way to the bridge, followed by Ray and B-10.

A few moments later, the small gunship appeared in the system of origin in time to see a white spacecraft with a black underbelly fly over the moon of a nearby planet. The missile of an attacking starcruiser destroyed an engine of an unknown entity.

"This is Surge, captain of the *Crimson Blade*. Cease your attack at once."

Surge's orders fell on deaf ears and the fleeing vessel continued to be bombarded by the gunfire of the attacking rocket-like starcruiser, which had a large ring encircling her stern. Hurtling towards the moon, the damaged ship disappeared under the moon's atmosphere.

The cruiser immediately opened fire at the *Crimson Blade*.

"B-10, return fire!"

The red ship dodged the shots from the unknown shuttle.

"Roger," said the monotone voice of B-10.

"Ray, see if you can find a weak point!" Surge commanded.

"Surge, that whole ship's a weak point." Ray had completed his scan of the unknown ship. "If we-"

Before Ray could finish, B-10 fired two blue particle rays at the enemy ship. The cruiser exploded in a spherical flash.

"What just happened?" Surge asked, in surprise.

"Like I was saying." Ray glared at their leader. "That ship had almost no shields and was-"

"SURGE!" Denise came onto the bridge.

As ship’s cook, Denise had not been present. She came up because no one had bothered to inform her of the reasons for the ship’s current movements.

"What's..." The brunette paused a moment upon seeing a display of the cruiser on Ray's screen. "I've seen one of those before!"

"You have?" Surge stood up.

"Where?" Ray remaining fixed on his screen.

"Back on the *Nomad*," she answered. "Each of the generational ships had one as a defense cruiser. The ship was only activated during the attack by the Koal slavers. What is that up there for?"

"That would mean the ship shouldn't have been able to break lightspeed," Ray commented. "But there was a crude FTL drive on the ship."

"You still haven't answered my question," Denise complained, crossing her arms.

"One of those ships opened fire on us," B-10 answered. "And as Surge ordered, I eliminated the target."

"What!" Denise let out a yell.

"It was self-defense!" Surge tried to explain.

"Distress signal coming from the surface!" B-10 interrupted.

"We are going down to the moon." Surge changed the subject. "Go make sure that Kira hasn’t decided to take a nap somewhere."

The *Crimson Blade* landed on a section of the moon covered in a violet forest. The crew, with the exception of Ray, exited the small gunship. Surge disembarked armed with the dragon hilted katana, which matched the color of his alien hair. Denise was armed with a single hooksword and an energy rifle. B-10 was holding a pair of compact submachine guns.

Kira needed nothing but herself.

"Why are the leaves of this place purple?" Denise examined the forest in amazement.

"It is a Lecara formed world," B-10 answered. "However, this world appears to have been abandoned. Could be that the noble in charge of managing this world was most likely forced into slavery or killed during the revolution."

So this is the kind of place that Surge's alien side comes from, Denise speculated. The end of Kira's catlike tail brushed her face. "Kira, watch it!" Denise started spitting the white fur out of her mouth.

"Sorry about that," the catgirl apologized with a smile.

"You know," Surge yawned, "I could really go for a peanut butter and chili pancake sandwich with mustard."

Dear Heavenly Father, forgive me, Denise prayed, *but I'm going to kill him if he even touches any food.*

The group came to a trail of crushed trees leading to the remains of a ship. Surge, Kira, and B-10 had never seen such a starship before, but Denise recognized the design type. Despite being torn in half, the black and white spaceship with no straight edges clearly appeared to be a transport shuttle for a *Nomad* class ship.

As they approached the crash site to investigate, they found the remains of the crew, all dressed in gray jumpsuits.

Denise prayed silently for the doomed crew before she saw something small and dark moving in the shadows. A pair of emerald green eyes with slit like pupils watched her.

"Hello there." Denise extended her hand towards the darkness.

"Denise, what are you doing?" Surge was ready to draw his weapon.

"Look, how cute she is." She grabbed the black bobtail kitten.

"Meow!"

"Surge!" yelled Ray's voice over Surge's handheld. "There's another-----atmosphere entr---"

"They must be jamming..." Surge went silent.

Looking to the red sky, they saw a spear-like object, with a black cable trailing behind it, dropping from the clouds. With a loud boom, a white plume of dust rose from the crater as the cable jerked back, holding firm. Mere moments later, a shallow cone slid down the wire in the sky.

Denise stuffed the kitten into her jacket. She closed the zipper.

"We're going to have company!" Surge activated his personal shield generator and drew his katana.

Denise and B-10 followed his lead, raising their guns before taking cover in the shuttle's broken hull.

Emerging from the purple and blue leaves were over a dozen men in jumpsuits with black armor covering their torso and upper arms. The uniforms were identical to those of the dead from the crashed ship. Each man was armed with a quad-barreled oblong shaped-rifle and wore a helmet with a blue tinted lens over his left eye.

The strange soldiers charged the broken craft, opening fire on those within. B-10 returned fire with a hail of needle-like rounds. Denise fired a blue energy beam at one of the men, which tore through his black armor.

While Surge charged in with his sword, cutting down two of their attackers, Kira lept from the wreckage and kicked one of the soldiers in the face, shattering his glass lens.

A large semihumanoid machine dropped down in front of them. Standing over 12 feet tall, its laser sights locked onto the four bounty hunters. A round fired at them, striking Surge's katana, snapping the blade in two.

"What do we do now?" Denise pointed her gun at the mech.

"How about asking that God of yours for a little help!" Surge replied.

The mouth of Surge's dragon hilt snapped open and fired out a half dozen pencil-sized mini-rockets at the robot. Denise fired a pulsating beam at the war machine's joints in a vain attempt to disable it. B-10's targeting system maintained constant fire on any missiles the mech attempted to launch.

Their efforts seemed to have little effect on the enemy robot as the machine inched closer and closer towards them. All hope seemed lost when, without warning, they heard the loud blast of a starship engine. The diamond shaped bow of the *Crimson Blade* plowed through the purple forest and rammed into the enemy mech, shredding the robot under her keel.

The small red ship swung towards them and the keel entry plank dropped down. B-10 grabbed Surge in her arms and Kira did the same with Denise, before jumping the 10 feet gap between them and the ship. Within a matter of seconds, they were all back on the bridge, each taking a seat.

"Blast that elevator cable and prepare to make the jump to dark space!" Surge ordered.

"All right," Ray replied.

A blue particle beam fired from the *Crimson Blade,* striking the orbital cable just under the clouds. The cable snapped spiraling downwards and striking the forest below like a whip. The red gunship zoomed past the second starcruiser and vanished into a starless pocket of space.

The four organic crewmen breathed a sigh of relief.

"What was all that about?" Kira stretched.

"I don't know," Surge closed his eyes.

"Before they jammed us, I was able to use B-10 as a relay point to hack the crash site," Ray explained. "They were carrying a selection of resurrected and modified extinct species. The shuttle crew was trying to steal these animals to become merchandise for the Auction of Worlds."

"I wish you would tell me when you start using our crewmen as relay points," Surge commented.

"Meow!" came from Denise's jacket.

"Hello there." She unzipped her jacket and the black bob tailed kitten jumped out.

"Meow!"

"Can't your brother's cat talk?" Surge looked down at the animal. "Is this one dumb?"

"I don't think cats talking is normal," Ray commented.

"Okay, Kira." Surge turned to the catgirl. "You translate."

"While my kind had some characteristics modeled after felines, my DNA is still in humanoid format." Kira swung her tail in annoyance.

"Guess we'll have to pay Karl a visit," Surge commented.

"Rendezvous point set," said B-10.

The kitten ran under one of the consoles.

Denise knelt down beside the cat.

"You have such pretty green eyes." She petted the cat. "I think I'll call you Emerald."

"Meow!"

Chapter 20- Encounter in Space

"It's good to have my proper arm back." Sophia flexed her restored left hand. "And that numbness is finally gone."

"It might still be sensitive and in need of recalibration." Gavin scanned over the arm with his monocle.

"It's fine." Sophia pulled her jacket on and left the workshop.

As she made her way down the corridor she felt a presence behind her, something watching her, following her. The wire around her left wrist uncoiled itself, ready to ignite.

Sophia spun around, ready to confront the presence behind her. But nothing stood in front of her.

"I'm here to escort you." She down looked to see Lightening swinging his tail back and forth. "Look, I understand the desire to try out the ancient feline punishment of denying Karl your presence, but if you keep this up he might forget to feed me."

"What? You've tried to punish Karl by not seeing him?" The wire rewrapped itself around her wrist. Having the cat leave them alone for an extended period sounded like a relief to her.

"I have thought about it. I suspect that those around me could only survive a nineteen hour absence from me before madness or death set in, just long enough for a catnap."

"I guess he would get lonely without me," she concluded, ignoring the existence of the rest of Karl's crew.

"Attention, all crew!" Zrela's voice broadcast. "A combat test between our newest crewman, Tut, and Reginia, will be commencing shortly in the mess hall. Get ready to place your bets."

The silence of the corridor was replaced by noise of drinking pirates sitting around the outer edge of a circle of tables with Reginia and Tut staring each other down in the center.

Zrela, as always, wore pants like a Terran woman, and was flirting with Karl's former classmates, Justin and Jacob, who displayed no interest. Meanwhile, Henry and Gavin were both competing for the attention of Alice.

Reginia removed her black coat, revealing the dark form-fitting armor underneath before placing it on one of the tables.

"Anyone who damages my coat will be walked down an air

lock." Reginia drew a black short sword from her side and Tut did the same.

Sophia spotted Karl with a bottle of coconut rum in front of him.

She skirted about the other pirates before sitting down beside Karl.

"Did you agree to this fight?" Sophia sat down beside him.

"No, but I didn't try to stop it, if that is what you are asking. As captain, I only insisted they not damage the ship."

Both fighters took a fencing stance and began thrusting their sword at each other.

Alarms rang throughout the ship.

"Captain." Miss Holo appeared above Karl's handheld. "The Oracle had detected an Evlon battle cruiser." The image of a teacher was replaced by an oblong space ship.

"Deploy point defense drones, lock turrets onto the vessel." Karl and Sophia made their way to the bridge. "Have the Oracle-"

"I hope you enjoy your reward," transmitted voice of King Bob. "I took the liberty of informing the Evlon Order of a certain artifact of the 'Great Elder Race', and they were most appreciative."

A swarm of diamond shaped drones launched from the starboard and port side before taking their place orbiting the ship. The Evlon ship fired several warheads at the *Nemesis.* The missiles were quickly annihilated by the red particle beams of the drones. Four orange beams fired from the *Nemesis'* two aft turrets, striking the attacking ship's bow.

A blue light emitted from the bow of the *Nemesis,* before streaking across the ship, causing the frigate to vanish.

Chapter 21- The Two Princes

A fleet of star-cruisers bearing the royal crest of the Titan Empire drifted parallel to a wall of gold and black warships three hundred million miles away.

Prince Alec of the Titan Empire was aboard the dreadnought, *HISS Kaiserin Alexandria Victoria*, which served as his flagship.

The officers were dressed in yellow-gold uniforms trimmed in silver. This style invoked a sense of superiority over the simple jumpsuits of Terran exiles that came before the Empire. There had always been a need to restore the beauty that was lost during humanity's first two world wars.

The crew watched their young blonde master move a ruby pawn forward.

"What are your thoughts on this?" The Terran adjusted his white cape as a holographic yellow topaz pawn slid forward.

"It's an interesting game but somewhat lacking," said the projection of the Lecaran commander.

"Well, it is a three thousand year old game from India." The Titan Prince's king side knight moved out.

"Where's that?"

"Part of South America, I think, it doesn't matter. If it was part of the British Empire then it belongs to Titan."

"Try telling that to the Neith Empire."

"You mean the Federation."

"I refuse to recognize those rebels." The Lecaran moved his knight over his pawns. "Once the monarchy is restored, the inner planets of Sol will remain under our control."

"Ulai-"

"That's Prince Ulai."

Ulai's flagship locked onto the Titan dreadnought.

"Now are we really going to switch games this soon?" Alec moved out his second knight. "And I was originally just going to ask about your thoughts on this Auction of Worlds."

"Yes, that." A yellow-gold pawn took a red knight. "Selling of the hand of lost royalty, such disgrace should be punished."

"They haven't said anything about selling the noble maiden."

Alec took Ulai's knight with his own. "And this criticism is coming from a prince who loans his fleet out to the highest bidder."

"It is a necessary evil in order to ensure that the Principality of Talon remains a home to all destitute nobles of the Neith Empire." Ulai castled on the king side. "If you went behind your grandmother's back and did the same, that colony of yours would already be a paradise."

"Her Majesty the Kaiserin of Titan Empire, England, Scotland, Byzantium, Canada, Germany, Australia, and Tzarina of Russia, would be most displeased with that betrayal of trust." Alec removed his cape and draped it over the back of his chair. "Even with my aunt and all my cousins in the way, there is always the chance the throne could fall to me or my descendants. And in the event that the lost noble woman is of authentic blood, I would not object to coming to her rescue. I wonder if she'd be to able to help with organizing my glassware collection."

"That sounds like an interesting challenge." Ulai smirked. "Depending on her race, she could be of value as ether bride or mistress. I think I shall retire for the night and continue this game in the morning." Ulai took a glass and raised it. "To your Terran reclamation."

"To the Second Neith Empire."

Ulai and the topaz chess pieces vanished, leaving Alec with his men.

"Your Highness do you really support a resurrection of the Neith Empire?" asked one of the officers.

"Of course. If the Neith fall into civil war again, then Earth will be more easily invaded by a joint Titan and Martian invasion. Mars will claim the Catholic territories and the Protestant sectors will fall to us."

"What about the other areas?"

"Well, hopefully the Pope or the owner of the Martian Throne will see reason at that time."

"Your Highness! We're detecting a Neith frigate crossing the battle line."

"What!?" Alec rose from his throne.

"Shall we open fire on Ulai's fleet?"

"Have the *Durandal* lock onto the blockade runner." A cruiser under Prince Alec's command targeted weapons at the stray frigate. "Hold-"

"What is the meaning of this?" Ulai's voice interrupted. "If you were going to attack me with a stolen ship, you should have at least had the decency to paint her in Titan colors."

"That ship isn't yours?"

"NO! That warship is part of the Neith Federation."

A few hundred miles away a large oblong ship appeared behind the frigate in a blue flash. The oblong ship launched a volley of missiles at the gold and black ship. The frigate returned fire with the orange beams of her four double turret.

"Open fire on the Evlon ship!" Both princes shouted upon seeing the inverse pentagram with Earth at its center.

The Evlon battleship's starboard side was bombarded by the missiles and railguns of the Titan fleet, while her port side was spammed by thousands of participial beams of every color known to man from the entity of Ulai's.

The smoking husk of the Evlon ship emerged from a cloud of debris after a full second of sustained fire. Both fleets waited for more ships from the Evlon sect to appear but none did.

"What should we do now?" Karl looked at the projection of each fleet on either side of his ship.

"Offer them a can of cat food." Lightening stretched across Karl's shoulders.

"Oracle, can you jump us out of here?" Ignoring the cat, Karl turned to where the Oracle had been floating, but instead, the gold disk just rolled on the floor.

"He says no." Lightening lept off Karl, pouncing on the gold disk.

"Attention unidentified entity," called a voice over the communication system. "This is Prince Alec of-"

"Attention, stolen vessel!" another voice interrupted. "This is Prince Ulai, of the Principality of Talon. Surrender at once!"

"Ulai, that ship is closer to my fleet than yours."

"But that ship is of my race and matches several of my

warships. It wouldn't look right with your ships."

"Hail them." Karl sat rubbing his forehead. "This is Captain Karl Sabers, in service to-"

"This doesn't concern you," Ulai interrupted.

"Then we will have to settle this with another match," Alec suggested. "Unknown Ship, if you attempt to flee before we have settled things, we will open fire."

The transmission ended and the entire crew of the *Nemesis* was totally lost in the surrealism of being the prize in some kind of gambling match.

"Captain." A projection of Miss Holo appeared in from of him. "Before you ask- No, the ship cannot get out of range under her own power. Weeeeeeee'llllllllllllllllllll."

Karl moaned.

"I wish she'd stop trying to use contractions, now we will have to reboot her too."

Chapter 22- The Stalling Princess

After what seemed like days, the two fleets finally sent their flagships towards the *Nemesis*. Boarding tubes extended from each of the larger ships.

Both Prince Alec and Prince Ulai received permission to come aboard from the apparent owner of the vessel.

"As I said, this is a starship which belongs to my family." Sophia glared at the two princes from the captain's chair. "Sadly due to hard times, I have been forced to crew my ship with an assortment of peoples."

Karl stood behind her.

"I think you're being insulted." Lightening whispered, firmly perching on Karl's shoulder.

"Lady Sophia, I wasn't aware you were among the nobles to escape the revolution." The Lecaran Prince kissed the hand of Sophia. "Perhaps I could arrange a sanctuary for you in exchange for your vessel."

"And I knew of a baron by the name of Ulai, but not of a prince by that name?" Sophia leaned back in the captain's chair.

"Well, certain steps had to be taken to establish a refuge for our people."

"Before you start making deals, might I remind you that I was the winner and we are still on the edge of my territory?" Alec glared at Ulai, before looking at Sophia. "How did you manage to get that Evlon ship tailing you, and what were you doing in my territory?"

"Unfortunately, we were attacked by an unprovoked Evlon battleship and had no choice but to flee."

"You know, this ship seems to match the description of a frigate that was rumored to have been stolen from the Neith Federation by a former noblewoman." Alec slowly scanned the bridge. "I was under the assumption that most of the Neith nobility was turned into slaves."

"I assure you this ship was built to serve my family." Sophia glanced down at the slave bracelet embedded her right wrist making sure that her sleeve still covered it. "This ship is in her rightful hands. I know that your empire still respects private ownership. My right under the Neith Empire entitles nobles with the rank of vassal to possess ships of war, provided they would assist the royal family in times of need."

"It is a great tragedy that my ships were prevented from leaving my system." Prince Ulai backed away slightly. "By the time my ships were ready, the royal family had been executed and the rebel government was established in the Sol System."

I guess technically she's not lying about the Nemesis being hers, however considering we both stole the ship, I would think I'm entitled to a least half of the frigate.

Karl watched on as Sophia stood up to both princes.

At least there was not any sign that they were looking to court her.

The Oracle disc, which had been placed on a bridge console, began to rise into the air slowly. Before anyone noticed, Lightening lept from Karl's shoulder and jumped on the saucer.

"You should probably stay out of the way until we need to leave." Lightening loomed over the Oracle like a lion ready to strike his prey.

"I suppose we could also add this ship as a prize for the one who rescues the lost noblewoman from the Auction of Worlds." Ulai glanced over at Alec.

"No, I won the game." Alec glared at Ulai.

"Yes, but that was before it was revealed that she was a displaced noble."

"So you two are also guests at the auction?"

"Yes, my lady." Ulai turned back towards Sophia. "The two of us both received the same invitation from a small ship that appeared in our territories."

"And would either of you happened to know the identity of this noblewoman?"

"Unfortunately no." Alec looked over at the young captain. "So far, my sources have not been able to identify the woman in question or even the background of this Charles Sanwell."

"I guess we will have to keep you here until the auction." Prince Alec left the bridge to return to his ship.

"It looks like we will be seeing each other again." Prince Ulai waived before exiting the bridge.

Lightening walked back over to Karl, freeing the Oracle to hover in the air.

"I'm not waiting here until the auction!" Sophia stood up and turned towards the Oracle.

"Do you think your uncle and his Syndicate friends could fence that ship?" Karl looked at the wreckage of the enemy vessel.

"I've taken the liberty of contacting Lord Baldassara." Miss Holo's image materialized on the bridge. "He would be most interested in collecting that vessel, and his compensations for her recovery would meet our estimated threshold for the auction."

"Before we meet up with him, maybe we should have Gavin and Alice see if we can swipe anything useful to our ships."

Several cables fired from the *Nemesis* into the bow of the decimated Evlon ship.

Both ships vanished in a single flash of light.

Chapter 23- Dress Up

Surge walked down the corridor eating a bowl of corn mixed with peanut butter, broccoli, bacon bits, topped with cheese and whipped cream, with a pickle on top.

Ray had informed him about a bounty that had something to do with the Syndicate, and that was enough to get him interested.

Surge heard Ray talking to the others, as he approached the small cargo hold of the *Crimson Blade.*

"…so the infiltrating the auction will be essential." Ray's voice became clearer as Surge approached the door. "The place will be swarming with guards and assassin machines if we make even the slightest misstep."

Surge walked in and saw an unforgettable sight. Standing there in front of Ray were both B-10 and Kira, dressed as maids.

"Wow! I didn't know you had a maid fetish." He patted the boy on the back while his eyes wandered around for Denise.

Ray balled up his fist.

"I don't!" He pointed at the girls. "This is what's necessary to capture Marth Greenbreath."

"Who's that again?" Surge scratched his head.

"Marth Greenbreath is one of the Five Lords of the Syndicate," B-10 explained. "Like Baldassara, he answers directly to the Triad. I wonder sometimes how you would do as a lone bounty hunter since you know nothing about the criminal underworld in the galaxy."

"Enough with insults." Surge scratched the metallic copper hair on the back of his head. "For a machine, you sure are critical. Where's Denise anyway? I've been itching ever since we picked up that mute cat."

"She's over there." Kira pointed at a metal crate sitting towards the back of the cargohold.

Kira! You little… thought Denise, who was hidden behind the crate.

Kira walked over to the crate and pulled Denise out from behind the metal box.

"No, Kira!" she yelled as the catgirl revealed Denise in her maid outfit.

"Here you go." Kira pushed Denise into Surge's arms.

Both of their faces turned red.

"I just detect a chemical reaction from Surge which would indicate arousal." The gynoid verbalized her observation.

Denise pushed herself away and threw a punch at Surge, who moved out of the way dodging her attack. Ray had B-10 put a halt to things before any blood could be spilled.

"You're next." Ray pointed to a folded black and white suit sitting on a crate. "You three leave, so Surge can change. Greenbreath will be at the Auction of Worlds along with Baldassara. They will be representing the Syndicate. For both the head of the Syndicate drug lords and the head of the pirates to be in one place at the same time means something very important to the Syndicate."

"What?" Surge looked down at the boy giving him orders. "I didn't sign up for that part. Why don't you go?"

"You have to." Ray looked sternly at the older bounty hunter. "We can't risk the pirates hacking our systems again. Also we'll need someone on the outside in the event something needs to be purchased legitimately."

Surge was then forced to disguise himself as a butler with the materials provided by Ray. When Denise saw him again, he was dressed in a black suit, with his hair dyed to match his clothes. In his hand he was carrying his new katana with his previous sword copper dragon hilt now attached. The four of them gathered by a mirror-like sphere large enough for them to climb in.

"Are we going to be doing something like dropping all of us on a planet inside that thing?"

Denise feared they were planning to do just that.

"Lord, I hope not." A feeling of discomfort came over Surge at the sight of the drop pod. "I still have nightmares about the last time we used it."

"I thought it was a very relaxing trip." Kira smiled.

"That is due to the concrete fact that your race was built for battle," B-10 explained in her usual monotone. "It is only logical that you would receive no discomfort from the drop."

"Unfortunately that won't work." Ray crossed his arms. "We'll have to try something a little more dangerous this time. The plan is to release the pod and have it attached to a ship entering into the VIP sections. Those attending the auction will likely assume that you are part of the staff at the auction. Those running the auction will believe that you are the servants of those likely to be high bidders."

"Why can't we cloak the ship and drop the pod on Sanwell's planet?" Kira was still hoping for her fun ride.

"That is because the system where the Auction of the Worlds is being held is mostly uncharted and we can't even be sure that it's on a planet," Ray answered. "Also you're going to be limited to chemical based projectiles weapons."

"What! You mean like those ancient pistols that Karl collects?" Denise hoped she would not get another history lesson about firearms.

"Yes." Ray pulled out a small box housing two short barrel revolvers and a small semi-automatic pistol. "I had the atomic printer produce these last night. I have to say the designs are brilliant. They are totally mechanical and require no power, but that does limit the revolvers to five shots. I was able to extend the semi-auto's rounds to seven by lowering the caliber."

"Doesn't Surge already have one of those?" Denise referred to the large revolver Surge often wore at his side.

She realized that Surge had never actually drawn his gun before.

"That's just a tool for a rainy day." Surge attempted to stick his long barrel revolver into his suit jacket.

"And that one has a power source. So, no you can't take it." Ray took the ivory hilted weapon from Surge's hand. "Any weapon that has a compact inertial dampener built into the handle is definitely going to show up on their tracking systems."

"What about B-10?" Surge looked over at the human-like robot.

"I can lower my internal voltage to approximately the electric charge of an organic nervous system." B-10 updated her companions. "However, while in that state I will be quite limited in my functions. My optical scanners will also be reduced to what Terran's approximate as 20/10 vision."

"I think we're being insulted." Surge looked over at Ray and

Denise, who were not too pleased with the comment either.

He took one of the two smaller revolvers while B-10 took the other, leaving Denise with the semi-automatic.

"Doesn't Kira get one?" Denise then remembered that Kira did not take a weapon on that moon.

"I am my own weapon. If I need a gun I'll just grab one off of the Syndicate thugs while we're there."

Kira stood up straight in front of Denise.

The Terran now noticed the catgirl had become slightly taller than she was before.

Chapter 24- The Arrival

Traveling towards a gigantic black pyramid-shaped object encircled by a flat gold ring was a long cylindrical ship with three stern mounted engines arraigned in a triangular form. Still in the process of repair, the *Lady Eris'* narrow central hull was partly open, with long temporary boarding tubes connecting the two sections of the ship covered by a yellow-orange forcefield.

The original pirate ship had been chosen to avoid recognition by the forces of the Neith Federation as well as the two princes they had run from. The Nemesis would remain hidden until needed.

Wearing a long sleeved silvery shirt with a gold cape and a large medallion that hung from his neck, Karl exited the ship. Hanging from a yellow-gold rope on his waist was his khopesh.

At his side was Sophia, wearing a silvery pale blue dress with poufed sleeves. The dress was almost perfectly symmetrical with the exception of her wrist. Her left sleeve stopped just before the wire around her wrist and her right sleeve extended into a triangle covering the top of her hand. A diamond shaped broach pen, doubling as a personal shield generator, was placed over her heart.

"I thought you said that I would look like a barbarian without a hat?"

"That is for Terran clothing," Sophia said. "Among my people it is not always a requirement."

It was never a requirement on the Nomad either, Karl thought.

"As a knight of the Second Neith Empire, I expect you to dress the part."

"Does this mean I'll get a full knighting ceremony?" Karl fantazied about being one of the knights of Ancient Europe dressed in shining armor with beautiful princesses and noblewomen at his side. He solemnly remembered that the elegance of Ancient Europe ended with First World War, which was followed by two mechanized centuries of darkness.

Some 1800 years later Karl, a descendant of veterans of that war, and Sophia, a beautiful creature beyond imagination, entered into a room with four other small spaceships, and at least fifty other people.

I hope my ancestors can see me now.

"I bet your ancestors are turning over in their graves," said Lightening.

"My ancestors are not buried in graves, cat," Sophia snapped.

"You are not the only one who had ancestors," Karl whispered.

"Everyone please move forward." A voice announced over the communication system.

"I was going to bring up my ancestor also." Lightening's tail wrapped around Karl's neck as the crowd pushed them.

"Later, cat. You better hold on or you'll soon be joining them."

Lightening clutched Karl's throat.

"Ow. Claws out of the jugular, please!" Karl looked around as more people disembarked. "They got a large turnout."

Two pale blue skinned humanoids made their way towards the couple with the cat.

Each Antarctican was dressed in a black uniform trimmed in gold. They resembled the form of a Terran or Lecaran but possessed glowing florescent irises. The woman's hair was a reflective black and she had yellow-gold irises. The man, with silvery white hair, had blue irises.

Karl noticed what was called the whites of his and Sophia's eyes were black on this man and dark red on the woman.

"Welcome to the *Auction of Worlds,"* the man spoke.

"Master Charles hopes you find something of interest," said the blue skinned female. "Everything here is for sale, including the ship."

The two then departed to greet the other guests.

"Sophia," Karl whispered. "What were those? Is this another alien race I'll have to deal with? Or is that what the Koal look like under their armor?"

"They're called Antarcticans," Sophia answered. "A three-way hybrid race of the Koal settlers who attempted to take the frozen pole of your homeworld, Terran slaves, and Lecaran criminals exiled by the Neith Empire. Their blue stained skin comes from the silver based blood of their Koal ancestors."

"So they're space Cajuns," Lightening commented. "Only they

are still on Earth. I'm glad I'm a cat. We all just mix together. No questions asked."

"This guy must have a lot of stuff if he's auctioning off this ship as well," Sophia observed.

The two of them began walking with a group of people into the room.

"An Inquisitor!" Karl pointed his gun at a gigantic suit of mechanical armor with white helmet and a body covered by a blue cloak draping from a pair of large pauldrons on each shoulder. Then he took a closer look at it, then kicked it lightly. "It's empty."

"Yeah, and if you break it, you buy it." The voice from behind them sounded familiar to Karl.

Karl turned to see John Madison.

"Karl! You're alive!" he let out in shock.

"I could say the same about you. Where is everyone?"

"Those of us taken by the Koal ended up here, after Sanwell found our ship-" John paused upon seeing the ruby eyes of Sophia. "Who is she?"

"Karl's space girlfriend," said the cat.

Well we did kiss, so that would make us more than just a princess and bodyguard, Karl thought.

"He can talk!" John exclaimed. "I know he was created from lost feline species but I wasn't expecting this!"

"Of course the talking cat is less believable than your childhood friend shacking up with a space alien," Lightening scratched his ear. "Typical human."

"WE ARE NOT SHACKING UP!" Karl and Sophia yelled in unison.

John grabbed the shoulder of his old friend and pulled him aside.

"You do know that her kind sent the Koal to conqueror Earth right?" John asked.

"Well it turns out that the Koal may have been just the initial wave." The Fall of Earth had become a new subject of historical interest to Karl since his separation from the *Nomad*. "Most evidence seems to indicate that the Neith forces did most of the conquering after the colonies left Earth's orbit."

"And why are you in league with her?"

"She needed my help." *And she is gorgeous*. "It's not her fault she's a descendant of the Ruby Eyed Empress."

"A child of the Ruby Eyed Empress? Are you mad?"

"Karl's xenophilia has resulted in many inconveniences," Lightening added. "But at least he's not into vampires. That's a whole mess that I'd rather not deal with."

"How many times do I have to tell you? I don't have a xenofetish!" Karl turned his attention back to his former classmate. "Relax. Once I help find her sister, we can all track down the *Nomad* and find a nice planet for all of them."

"Them?" John noticed Karl's use of *them* instead of *us*. "You plan on staying with this new Ruby Eyed Empress even after we reunite with our original colony ship?"

"Well-"

"Mr. Madison, have you finished your assignment?" Miss Holo's voice interrupted from Karl's handheld computer.

"I'm sorry Miss Holo!" John Madison jolted upon hearing that voice. "The alien blew up my-" he paused. "I not a student anymore and I have more important things to deal with than homework."

Karl pulled out his handheld and the image of Miss Holo appeared above the device.

"I was hoping that my students would endeavor to continue their studies even while in exile." The teaching program expressed is disappointment. "At least, Karl has maintained his study of history."

"John!" A blonde woman called as she approached. "Karl!"

Karl instantly recognized Denise's friend, Brittany, from the academy.

"Did you ever find Denise?" she questioned, still in shock over the reunion. "What happened to Justin and Jacob?"

"Well Justin and Jacob are part of my crew now," Karl answered. "And Denise is-"

"-is trying to run the life of the half-alien bounty hunter she lives with." Lightening licked his paw.

"Humanity has two perfectly fine empires now," proclaimed another man.

Karl turned to see the same man from the hologram

conversing with Sophia.

"Hello, I believe I have already made my introductions." Charles stretched out his hand to shake.

Karl noticed a gold and brass gauntlet adorned with jewels.

"You shake it." Charles looked down at his hand. "Ah, I forgot to take this thing off." He pulled off the gauntlet. Failing to stuff it into his back pocket, he shoved it into his jacket.

"Charles! Charles! There you are!" called a young woman's voice. "I've been looking all over for you!"

"And what is the problem?" Charles turned around to see a woman walking over to him.

Karl and Sophia were completely bewildered by the woman's shabby appearance accented by a red t-shirt, worn denim pants, and plastic flip-flops.

"There's this guy who's asking a lot of questions about one of the Evlon Lancers," said the woman.

"Paige, I would like you to meet Karl Sabers, captain of the *Nemesis*," he introduced them. "And?"

"Lightening, Grand Holy Emperor of the Known and Unknown Universe," proclaimed the cat perching proudly on Karl's shoulder.

"Of the what?" Paige looked closely at the cat.

Sophia glared at the feline, before turning to what looked to her like an impoverished slave.

How did they know about the Nemesis? Karl wondered. *We didn't even come in that ship.*

"I am Lady Sophia Rubyeyes." She curtsied.

Paige shook her hand.

"Cool. As you already know, I'm Paige Sanwell," she reintroduced herself.

"I've seen your kind in the historical data bases." Karl remembered the time he had to study the centuries following the first two world wars on Earth. "You're a hippie."

"I am not. This is high class outfit from Earth late 20th and early 21st centuries."

"People really used to dress like that?" Sophia leaned over to Karl.

"Indeed," Karl whispered. "That was how mankind dressed in the days before the Fall of Western Civilization."

"Your race deserved to be conquered." Sophia pulled away from Karl as Charles made his return.

Charles leaned over to the Terran woman and whispered something in her ear.

"This is my sister, Paige," Charles introduced her. "Vice president in charge of the auction."

"Hi! It's nice to meet you!" Paige smiled.

"Now, who's asking about the Lancer?" Charles rolled his eyes towards his sister.

"Ashley Claymore," she informed them. "He also wants to see you about that business deal you had with him."

Karl cringed at the mention of that name. Karl would have been happy to never again see the old crook who shanghaied him.

"Tell him yes. Never mind, I'll go tell him. You guys wait right here." Charles Sanwell left, departing into the crowd.

"I really don't want to meet Claymore again." Karl wondered how many more men and women had been shanghaied by that man.

"Yeah," Lightening agreed. "You don't want to get knocked out again."

"Lightening." Karl glared down at the feline. "You don't want to miss out on your can of tuna, do you?"

Karl looked around for John and Brittany. But they had disappeared with the mastermind of the auction.

"I'm starting to think the space princess is a bad influence on you." Lightening looked at Sophia, who stared daggerously back at him.

As they continued looking around at the displayed items, a familiar looking young boy charged towards them. Before Karl could properly react, the child, who appeared to be less than ten, kicked him in the shin.

"Mreooww!" Lightening hissed at the boy.

"Ow!" Karl let out clutching his leg. "What the hell was that for?"

Sophia stepped back. The wire around her left wrist uncoiled and ignited into a blade of plasma.

"I might not be able to collect the bounties on your heads at the moment." The boy stared at Karl and Sophia. "But in the name of Berry Lane, I have avenged myself."

A hooded Lecaran woman with a blue monocle over her left eye and a rapier at her side walked towards the boy. She karate chopped him in the head before making her way towards the princess.

"I am Ishtana, a humble bounty hunter, and I apologize for the actions of my partner." Ishtana took Sophia's hand and kissed it. "He is currently the latest in a series of clones that didn't quite mature as expected. It is an honor to see a member of the old nobility after all these years. Though I must say that it is odd to see your slave dressed as a knight of Neith."

"So now Karl's the slave." Lightening wiped his face with his paw. "Oh, how the tables have turned."

"Did that creature just talk?" The lady bounty hunter scanned Lightening with her monocle.

"Again, with space people questioning the talking cat." The annoyed feline walked around behind Karl and Sophia.

"I'm afraid I will have to leave you for a moment." Ishtana bowed to Sophia. "Our client would prefer that we not leave them unattended too long."

Ishtana then followed the young Berry Lane before disappearing from site.

"Attention all patrons!" announced the voice of Paige over the intercom. "The auction will begin shortly, please make your way to the main auction room."

The crowd made its way as instructed to a large amphitheater similar to the one Karl had seen when he had been sold off to the Evlon cult by the *Lady Eris'* previous captain. A rotating holographic image of the displayed auction item hovered above the center of this chamber.

The image of Charles Sanwell appeared and a circle of small gavels began orbiting him.

"And here we have an example of a phone." The image of an ancient communication device with a rotating dial of numbers and an elegant looking receiver was displayed. "These were once used to contact home to home in real time through a wired network back in the early age of mechanization."

"I've seen those before in a museum," Karl commented. "I think people replaced them with a form of handheld telegraph computers, despite the fact that they had wireless audio available."

"You mean like the thing they had in *Titanic*?" Sophia asked, "I thought that was just made up."

"No," Karl answered. "The *Titanic* was a real ship. I think she was the first in an era where cruise ships constantly sank, like the *Lusitania, Andrea Doria,* and the *Britannic, Titanic's* younger sister. Though if I remember correctly, Titanic's older sister, the *Olympic,* ran over and sank a submarine. Course that was a century of constant war so that makes sense."

"I thought the *Titanic* was a myth like King Arthur, Superman, Lt. Sinclair Plate, and that short guy who tried to conquer Earth before the development of space travel."

"Napoleon? No he was real and he wasn't actually that short, at least not for that time."

"No, I was talking about the one with the square mustache."

"Going once, going twice, sold for 9,000,000 Titan Cronos!" The auction for the phone concluded with the sound of gavels clacking in unison. "Next up we have the complete *Lt. Sinclair Plate in Sand Waves* series signed by the original author, starting at 60,000."

A man in the audience raised his hand.

"Do I hear 65,000?" A woman raised her hand. "Do I hear 70,000? Going once, twice, sold for 70,000 Titan Cronos. Up next we have the Worshiping Kitty." The image of a toy cat appeared. "This toy served as a companion to those without access to felines during dark times." The toy cat then raised itself from sitting to begging and began letting out a robotic meow. "Starting at 45,000 Titan Cronos."

Karl raised his hand. Sophia's eyes widened in reaction to Karl's purchase, and Lightening flicked his tail back and forth.

"45,000, do I hear 50,000?" Another man raised his hand.

"70,000!" shouted a woman.

"75,000!" The man jumped up.

"80,000," Karl let out.

"90,000!" yelled the man.

"100,000." Karl bid.

"100,000, do I hear 150,000?" Paige waited a few seconds for a second bidder. The gavels clacked together. "Going once, twice, sold for 100,000 Titan Cronos. Congratulations!"

The spherical transportation pod drifted into the maintenance area. It traveled into a hanger where the crew of the *Crimson Blade* disembarked and separated into pairs.

Surge and Denise went one direction while B-10 and Kira went another.

Denise noticed something out the corner of her eye as she and Surge sneaked down a corridor.

Two men in blue robes with black collars appeared coming towards a chamber. Another set of men in black robes with white collars came from the opposite direction.

However, before Denise had a chance to ponder the purpose of the blue robes, Surge immediately pulled her away by her wrists.

She turned to Surge who had suddenly become deathly pale upon seeing the second group of people.

"Are they mad?" Surge asked under his breath. "Putting those two factions in the same room together?"

"What's the matter?" Denise whispered.

"This place is about to turn into a bloodbath, and may very well start an intergalactic war!"

The group of seven then disappeared behind a set of double doors.

"Claymore! This wasn't part of the deal." Charles stood just outside the door to the private auction. "You didn't say anything about bringing them into this."

"Relax," said Ashley Claymore, holding his wooden cane with a dragon's head. "It's just a matter of who's going to pay the most."

Chapter 25- A Princess Revealed

"Lady Sophia, Captain Sabers." The blue skinned woman tapped Karl on the shoulder. "Your presence has been requested at a private auction."

Karl and Sophia rose from their seats and turned to follow the woman.

Concerned that he might miss out on an artifact of personal interest, Karl placed the Oracle disk in his seat for the purpose of monitoring the auction.

It was not long before they noticed several others being led away from the main auction. Among which was a Neith man with long metallic silver hair and ruby red eyes.

Karl immediately recognized Baldassara. Beside him was a middle-aged man with bright red hair, clad in a dark green coat.

Two others stood out. A Neith man wore a similar outfit to the one worn by Karl. And a Terran man was dressed in a pale yellow uniform with silver trim, a purple sash, and a white cape.

The group was escorted to a chamber where each guest was seated along the outer rim of a table with the shape of a crescent moon. Anchoring opposite ends of the table were two pairs of men in robes, already seated.

Karl recognized one of each set. In a black robe, on the right end of the table, was Father Gabriel, the halfbreed priest. And on the left hand side was Kordova, another old man Karl had hoped not to encounter again.

Father Gabriel's companion echoed his attire while Kordova and his partner wore blue robes.

Karl's thoughts quickly changed to escaping with Sophia, knowing full well the hatred Kordova's sect had for humanoid aliens.

"Welcome, honored guests." Charles looked somewhat nervous despite having a calm tone in his voice. "Would you like to introduce yourselves before we get started?"

"I am High-Theorist Kordova," the old man with a long beard said. He glanced at the other man in a blue robe. "And this is my assistant."

"I am Father Gabriel," the young man introduced himself,

before glancing over at the older priest in a black robe with his red eyes. "And this is Father Abraham."

"Admiral Dalia of the Neith Federation," announced the Neith woman with blackening metallic silver hair. She wore a blue dress with black cuffs and high collar.

A yellow gem dangling from the lady admiral's belt turned from yellow to red and Dalia’s eyes locked onto Sophia.

"Prince Ulai."

The prince stood up.

"Current head of the Principality of Talon, former vassal of-"

"We've heard enough, Mercenary Prince," said the other figure in blue robes. "You don't need to give your hero BS about surviving the fall of the Neith Empire."

"This coming from the people who tried to drop the Phobos onto Mars in the name of freeing humanity from the chains of an archaic religion." Dalia glanced at Kordova. "Personally, both of you should be sent away to melt on the surface of Venus. As for the rest of you Red Bloods, the only solution to your violence is complete subjugation."

"Those were the action of Blood Terra, not the Evlon Temple," Kordova defended. "While we do share similar views on the obsolete religion and the false copies of humanity that have taken our mother world, we had no part in the failed attempt to drop Phobos onto New Vatican City."

"And I am Prince Alec, Duke of Osiris." A Terran man dressed in a silver trim uniform locked his eyes onto Karl and Sophia. "Let’s put aside the incident that gave Mars its beautiful ring system, and attend to the matter at hand."

"I have to agree with the Titan prince." Baldassara was demanding the respect of the others in the room. "Lord Greenbreath and I have come a long way with the promise of a civilized purchase regarding items that each of us would find of value."

"And finally we have Karl Sabers and the Lady Sophia." Charles wiped his brow. "To begin with, we have a once in a lifetime opportunity. Starting at 1,000,000,000 we are offering the royal hand in marriage of the princess of a lost kingdom, and will have the honor of restoring her people."

"You can't be serious!" Sophia expected to see them bring her her sister to be auctioned off.

"I'm very serious." Charles smiled at Sophia. "This young princess will do whatever it takes to restore her people. Your Highness, if you would greet our guest."

Sophia's anxiety quickly faded into disappointment as Karl's blood pressure went up upon seeing a young Asian woman in a white dress. And not just any Asian woman either, but Yuki Amato, a girl who had been friends with Karl and Denise on the *Nomad*.

Yuki still wore the same beaded wedding dress with pouffed sleeves she had worn at the costume party, which occurred the day of the attack on the *Nomad*.

Her eyes widened in surprise as they met Karl's.

She remained silent.

"Princess Yuki's people spent generations in space seeking a new home after the invasion of Earth when they were attacked by marauders in deep space," Charles explained.

What is she doing here? Where is everyone else? Karl thought to himself. Yuki was never part of any nobility on the *Nomad.* However, if Karl spoke out about it could lead to more trouble.

"The princess's lineage can also be traced back to the Japanese royal family as well as the great Terran conqueror, Genghis Khan."

Well, she might have a relation to Genghis Khan same as any Europeans might be descended from Charlemagne, but she has just as much of a relation to the royal family of Japan as I would have to the Emperor Karl I of Austria-Hungary or the English monarchs.

"Do you have proof that she and her people are the ones that you claim they are?" Prince Alec tapped his fingers on the table.

"Yes." Charles pulled two glass vials of red liquid from his coat, each divided into three sections. "These contain DNA samples from Princess Yuki and two of her people." He slid one to Father Abraham and the other to Kordova.

Each of the old men pulled out a green monocle device and scanned the vials.

"The last time we were promised the lost children of Earth, it resulted in the loss of one of our most sacred artifacts." Kordova glared at Karl.

"Yes, and you didn't kill the previous captain of the *Lady Eris*." Lightening's sarcastic voice startled all in the room.

"Who said that?" Kordova exclaimed, rising from his seat.

"I did." Lightening jumped onto the table.

"Lightening!" Karl and Yuki yelled.

"If complaints are to be raised against my human, then it is my duty as his master to provide him with a defense." Lightening arched his back.

"Cat, he is my acting knight," Sophia informed Lightening.

"I've known him for far longer than you have." Lightening walked onto Karl's lap. "And if you adjust for cat time my time with him is seven times what you've known him, plus the time I met him before you woke up."

Ignoring the argument between the cat and the alien girl, Father Gabriel turned to Karl.

"Are you really from one of the lost colonies?"

"Yes," Karl answered. "And so is Yuki, we were both from the same generational ship."

"Can we get back to business?" asked the two older men.

The two princes snickered at the others while Yuki stood dazed by all that transpired around her.

"This has been very enjoyable." Prince Alec raised his right hand. "I'll go ahead and I'll bid 1,000,000,000 for the hand of Princess Yuki."

"Do I hear 1,500,000,000?"

The Kordova pulled a thick gold disk with crystal in its center from his robes. He placed it on the table.

"This is the map that the pirate, Micalo, wanted in exchange for the location of the lost colony," said Kordova's companion. "It should be well worth that. I assume you also have the location of the others."

"I'm not sure what that is for!" Charles was puzzled by the item's presence. "But we're not running on a barter system."

"It could be an acceptable form of payment." Another old man stepped into the room. "My name is Ashley Claymore, I am an associate of Charles and I'll be happy to cover whatever items you wish to exchange if they are equal value."

"I guess that would be acceptable," Charles somewhat reluctantly backed down, as Claymore took over the smaller auction.

"Where are the others from this colony?"

"We'll bring the other three once payment has been received."

"Then we'll take the colonist and be on our way." Kordova stood up ready to leave.

"Not so fast." Claymore turned towards the Father Abraham. "Let's see what you've got."

"Neither of us could take her hand in marriage." The old priest pulled a bag from inside his robes. "I am sure a suitable candidate could be found among the nobles of the Imperium." He opened up the bag, dumped the contents onto the table revealing a pile of stones, which glowed with a thousand colors. "You could buy a whole fleet with that. I assume you also have the location of the others."

"Indeed I do," answered Claymore. "As well as the destination of the colony ship which departed Earth. With that you might even be able to track down this entire lost colony from your home world."

"Are those radioactive?" Lightening looked at the gems.

"You know where the *Nomad* is?" Yuki immediately turned to Claymore.

"Keep quiet!" Ashley snapped at the fake princess.

"I will not allow you to speak to a lady in such a manner," Alec spoke up.

"If this woman is indeed a princess you have no right to speak to her with such disrespect." Prince Ulai crossed his arms. "And if she's not of noble blood then you are a fraud and should be cut down at once."

"So you know the locations of both the *Nomad* and the students." Karl glared at Claymore. Without thinking, the pirate captain turned towards Charles and raised his hand. "I'll pay the worth of those gems plus another 500,000,000."

"Karl!" Sophia pulled his arm back down, dragging Karl over to her. "We can't afford that."

"Can't it be paid out once your monarchy is restored," Karl whispered back.

The fear in Sophia's ruby eyes warped to one of jealousy as her gaze turned towards the Terran woman, someone who appeared to be a princess of Karl's own kind.

One he had known before her. One he might go back to.

"The Second Neith Empire is going to start off in debt." Lightening scratched his ear. "This better not come out of my cat food money."

"I'll match the value of those gemstones and add another 1,000,000,000." Prince Alec looked directly at Yuki. "In fact, my castle is currently in orbit about a newly terraformed world just waiting for a new colony to be established. What better way to establish a colony than with one of the lost tribes of Old Earth? If you and your people are willing to swear allegiance to the Titan Empire, I will ensure your liberation from whatever unscrupulous agreement Sanwell and his associates have forced you into."

"She's all yours, Titan." The mercenary prince leaned back. "I might be open-minded enough to have a Terran for a concubine but to marry one would not be fit in my position."

"Sold to Prince Alec of the Titan Empire." Charles concluded the auction for Yuki's hand. "Next up we have-"

"You can't just close it now!" Claymore turned to Sanwell choking his cane.

Sophia hid a smile of relief as Yuki's life passed into the hands of a Titan prince.

The whole room jolted.

"What was that?"

"This is Pride King Bob," broadcasted a man's voice. "There is currently a pride traitor among your guest. Surrender to us at once or my forces will destroy this station."

"This is Charles Sanwell, you are welcome to join us for the Auction of Worlds. I'm sure there is something for sale that would interest you, otherwise I request that you withdraw at once."

The whole room shook again with another broadside of particle beams striking the defense shields.

"I had hoped to save this one for last." Charles let out a disappointed sigh. "As I have a duty to protect my guests. I'm sure you will all be willing to act as witness that this is self-defense. Selina, fire up the weapon!"

Projected in front of them was a holographic model of the

pyramid ship surrounded by a fleet of cargo freighters and star yachts, which had been converted to gunships. The smaller ships continued firing beams as the ring surrounding the pyramid began to glow red, then orange, and finally white, before erupting with a pulse of lightning bolts that wrapped around every uninvited vessel in sight. When the bolts of lightning vanished, King Bob's ships simply drifted silently.

The guests sat in their seats dumbfounded.

"Now starting at 1,000,000,000,000!" Charles retook control of the auction. "We have the *Star Fleet Crusher,* a battleship capable of disabling within a quarter light second. And as a bonus, the ships caught in her attack can be recovered and added to your own forces with little repair."

"Where in Tartarus did you find this weapon?" Prince Alec exclaimed.

"Who said anything about finding her?" Charles smiled.

"You're claiming this ship as something of your own creation?" Kordova cut his eyes sharply at the two merchants. "The architecture of the vessel is clearly that of the Elder race."

"Huh?" Charles glanced over at Claymore.

"It is true that parts of the vessel may have been have been incorporated from the ruined remains of an unidentified object," Claymore explained, "but I assure you that this battleship's weapon systems are totally original."

"I think we've heard enough lies!" Kordova rose from the table and left the room, followed by his companion.

"I am sorry to hear that he was displeased with our private auction," Charles commented.

"Good riddance." Prince Alec ran his hand threw his blonde head of hair. "I really don't like those people. Now on behalf of Her Majesty, I bid the 1,000,000,000,000."

"Do I hear 1,500,000,000,000?" asked Charles.

The older priest raised his hand.

"Do I hear 2,000,000,000,000?" Charles turned to Dalia.

"You're happily willing to disrupt the galactic stability for the sake of money." The admiral looked at the two men with suspicion.

"It's been standard practice for ten thousand years among both your race and mine." Claymore shifted his gaze, looking towards Prince Ulai. "No reason to do away with something that works."

"2,500-"

"3,000,000,000,000. Merchant of Death," Dalia interrupted. "Let it be known if this weapon of yours is fake, you shall be hunted down and banished to the surface camps of Venus."

Charles swallowed and Ashley remained unfazed.

"I assume you know not to incur the wrath of my grandmother. 4,000,000,000,000." Prince Alec smiled at his new bride-to-be. "But I assume you're smart enough not to defraud the Titan royal family."

Yuki smiled nervously back.

"6,000,000,000,000." Father Abraham raised his hand.

Chapter 26- Explanations

"Karl."

The captain felt a tap on his shoulder and turned to see Yuki standing there in her white dress.

"What happened to you? And Denise? Is she still alive? Why did they call you captain? And who was the girl with gold hair?"

Yuki's questions came without hesitation on the part of the former student.

"Denise is fine, but the rest is complicated."

Karl was not quite sure how he was going to explain everything-

How Sophia was descended from the Rubyeyed Empress, the tyrant they had been raised to fear.

How he had become a pirate in his failed attempt to rescue his sister.

How his sister was now the cook to a half-alien bounty hunter.

How he planned to help Sophia find her sister and restore their empire.

How he was legally Sophia's owner, despite the fact that she ran his life.

How he was now in a relationship of sorts with Sophia.

Not to mention Lightening's ability to talk.

Plus, his theft, of not only a small alien ship, but also an entire frigate.

Plus he just bought another alien in a skirt named Tut.

In addition, he had just spent 100,000 Titan Kronos on a toy cat.

Moreover, he had made enemies of not only a clan of warrior aliens but a violent alien-worshiping sect of humans, which somehow hated all humanoid aliens as well.

Plus, he and Sophia shared the captain's quarters on his ship.

Finally, Justin and Jacob also shared a cabin.

Best not to tell her anything.

Maybe I can change the subject.

"Why did they call you-"

"Karl!" Sophia's voice sent a chill down Karl’s spine. "Would you mind introducing me to this royal friend of yours?"

"This is Yuki Amato." Karl spun towards Sophia, who stood right behind him. "She was a friend of mine and Denise's, back on the *Nomad*."

"You mean she was your old girlfriend," Lightening added.

Sophia looked like she was about to say something when the two Princes, Alec and Ulai, approached.

"It is a pleasure to meet you." The Titan prince kissed Yuki's hand. "Rest assured, your people will be given safe refuge on a new settled planet within the Ra System." Alec looked at Sophia and Karl. "So why is a Terran man dressed as a Neith soldier, when his loyalty should be directed at the monarch of his own people?"

"He is serving as my knight during my time in exile." She locked arms with Karl. "Who he was before coming into my service is of no importance."

"Lady Sophia, I am still curious how you managed to escape the revolution." The Lecaran Prince kissed the hand of Sophia.

"Ulai the Mercenary Prince of Talon." Baldassara appeared from the chamber with Nara coming to his side. "A former vassal who loans out his fleet and soldiers to the highest bidder. In a way you're not too dissimilar to Sanwell and his auction."

"Sadly the events of the revolution required my system to reorganize itself into a principality for the moment." Prince Ulai picked up a glass from a waitress attending to the needs of the patrons. "We were fortunate that enough of our imperial fleets remained loyal for us to maintain control of our system. I would be most interested in allying forces with that of another surviving noble house."

"An alliance could be beneficial to us." Baldassara took a drink for himself. "Between the forces of the Syndicate and Principality of Talon."

"Didn't he want you to steal Ulai's fleet?" Karl leaned over to Sophia.

"Yes, but if we are going to rebuild my empire we're going to need to make use of potential allies and vessels."

Chapter 27- Conspirators

"You would have been better off if you had just come as a guest instead of as an attacker." Charles looked at the restrained King Bob from across his desk. "But your appearance did give me the chance to test out my *Fleet Crusher*."

"I want the head of Lrakian calling himself Tut, his owner the upstart pirate, and the pirate's slave woman. Perhaps I can make you an offer?"

"We can discuss the member of your race but Captain Sabers and his Neith woman are already spoken for." Claymore entered the room with Admiral Dalia, and his servant, Isabella, following behind him. "Assuming they brought him with them on the ship, we can come to an arrangement. I understand the cultural importance of eliminating any threat to your rule. One must destroy the sons and bed the wives and daughters of your fallen enemy."

"And here I was worried that you only consorted with the wrong type of Lrakians." The cat-eared man glared at the woman with a wolf-like tail, before returning his attention to Dalia. "I assume the other party will dispose of those two for me? I guess those two must have angered more than just my pride and the Evlon loonies."

"The Federation's business is its own concern." Dalia gripped the hilt of her sword. "All that matters is those two are criminals who must be dealt with."

"And of course, Kordova people will be happy to have their Oracle back," Charles speculated. "But I'm not sure how receptive they'll be after what happened with the private auction."

"Oh, the bid on Karl Sabers' life is limited to just the admiral woman and the Evlon forces?" King Bob broke free of his restrains.

Charles and Dalia drew their weapons, and Isabella readied herself for combat.

King Bob merely placed his hand behind his back and kicked his feet up on Charles' desk.

"You lower races are so easily startled." The Lrakian man smiled at them. "But if you cannot provide me Karl Sabers, then I require another of his allies. The female pride defector working as a bounty hunter known as Kira. I believe she is working with some halfcaste bounty hunter with a red ship."

"I suppose that could be arranged." Claymore glanced at Sanwell.

"I'll be on my ship until you have retrieved the pirate and his woman." Dalia rose from her seat. "I would gladly handle things myself but that would only accelerate the coming wars."

Unbeknownst to Claymore and Sanwell, Kira and B-10 were listening behind the closed door.

"Shall we warn Denise's brother of this pending threat to him and his crew?" The gynoid's monotone expressed no sense of urgency.

"Contact Surge first. Let him know that King Bob is here." Not wanting the Lrakian king to know of her presence, she began sneaking away, with B-10 following close behind.

The door slid open and Dalia exited the room.

Kira and B-10 stood with up straight as though ready to be of service.

The admiral glanced at them as she walked down the corridor, but spoke not a word.

Chapter 28- Attacked

As Karl picked up his Worshiping Kitty from the humanoid robot at the counter, he heard the sound of gunfire behind him.

Is Lightening that jealous? He turned around half expecting to see his cat with a pistol, but instead a blonde Terran man stood there pointing a gun in the air, which was the size of a pistol, but fired countless rounds like a submachine gun. There were about twenty other men carrying the same type weapons and every one of them a Terran dressed in a blood red uniform.

Blood Terrans! Karl reached for his weapon, then he felt something cold touch the side of his neck. *Are they with Kordova?*

"Where is your captain?" A young woman with dark brown hair had one of the machine guns pointed at Karl's neck. The woman reached in Karl's vest and took his pistol.

"Alien scum," the blonde man called out. "Line up against the back wall!"

All of the non-Terrans did as instructed, except for Calidi and Ellris who were standing in the same place looking at each other. Ellris ran his hand through his silver hair. Calidi shook his head, then ran his finger along his nose. Ellris nodded and they both pulled short handled halberds from behind their coats, with glass axe blades and spearheads mounted on top of the short handles.

One of the terrorists came within three feet of Ellris and the handle of his weapon extended, piercing the chest of the terrorist with its spearhead. The other terrorist opened fire on the halberd welding fighters, who jumped out of the way in time to dodge the bullets. Four more terrorists fell to their blades a few seconds later.

While the terrorists were distracted, the wire around Sophia's left arm uncoiled into a gun and she hid behind a table turned on its side. She pressed down on her diamond shaped brooch, which activated her personal shield generator. Several of the hostages followed her example and opened fire on the enemy. Sophia fired three glowing shots into a Blood Terran's chest.

Seeing her comrade gunned down, the dark-haired woman turned her weapon towards Sophia. With a gun no longer pointed at his neck, Karl pulled his khopesh from his belt. The sickle sword turned orange with the activation of its charge-cutter and severed the girl's right arm before she had a chance to squeeze the trigger.

The disarmed woman quickly fled. Two other men each drew boxcutter-like handles from their belts. A pair of rods extending from the handles were quickly coated in green plasma.

Karl grabbed his light buckler as two other men came at him. He blocked one of the oncoming energy blades with his sword and the other was deflected by the pulsating forcefield coming from his buckler. A yellow bolt fired into the torso of the attacker on Karl's right, freeing his sword hand to slash the stomach of the man on his left.

Karl glanced over to see Sophia standing behind a column with her plasma coil forming a gun in her synthetic hand. Karl ran towards Sophia as another attack with an axe came at him. Karl's plasma derringer extended from under his left sleeve and fired at the axeman's head.

Only three of the terrorists, including the woman who had confronted Karl, managed to get away. The rest were massacred by the pirate crewmen, armed nobles, and their body guards.

Karl found Sophia sitting behind the table.

"You all right?" Karl pull Sophia to her feet.

"I think so." She dusted herself off with her right hand as the coil rewrapped itself around her wrist.

"I knew things would go south as soon as Kordova and Claymore showed," Karl commented.

"You should have realized that nowhere on this plane of existence is safe," answered Lightening, who had been absent the entire time. "Your only hope of survival is to provide me offerings of ham and tuna."

"It's not unheard of for Blood Terra to attack non-Terran even on a properly governed world," answered Sophia. She looked down at the cat. "And where were you, Lightening?"

"The noise was bothering me, so I left."

"Captain," said Calidi, "I would advise we return to our ship and get Her Highness to safety."

"All right," Karl sheathed his weapon. "Strip the terrorist bodies of anything valuable!"

Several of the hostages, who did not take part in slaughtering the terrorists, made their way towards the door, but were quickly blocked by the crossed halberds of Calidi and Ellris.

"What are you doing?" Karl asked.

"We currently lack sufficient crew," Calidi informed him. "We intend to correct that problem."

The ship jolted again.

"I thought that super weapon took out the Lrakian ships!" said Karl.

Lights began flashing all across the pyramid ship housing the auction.

"Captain." The voice of Miss Holo came from Karl's handheld. "There are no active external enemies nearby. But this vessel has sustained heavy damage."

"Can we get to the *Lady Eris*?"

"Negative. The *Lady Eris,* along with several other vessels, were decoupled by the explosion." The image of the *Lady Eris,* and a dozen other ships drifting away, appeared above Karl's handheld before being replaced by the image of a blue sun. "I regret to inform you but this ship is on a collision course with the nearby star."

"I've already had one of my lives endangered by a sinking ship. I failed to see why I needed to be on another doomed ship." Lightening's tail swung side to side.

"Why isn't anyone coming back for us?" Sophia leaned over the pocket computer.

"Sanwell's weapon appears to have taken out the ships that were docked with this one as well. There are smaller ships inside but they aren't large enough to accommodate everyone," Miss Holo reported.

Karl spoke up. "Miss Holo, get ahold of Denise and the *Crimson Blade.* Have them send over Ray. And can you or the Oracle get in contact with *Nemesis?"*

Karl took notice of a dark-haired man and a blonde among those detained by Sophia's bodyguards. *I guess I'll have to try commandeering this ship, too. I can do it. I've got my courage, my crew, and my cat!*

"John! Travis! I'm going to need you to bring me to your boss so we can clear things up."

"We didn't know anything about this." John swallowed. "All I heard was that he would be meeting with the Barley People."

"Who are they?" Karl adjusted his grip on the sword.

"We don't know. Claymore and Sanwell never told us." Travis backed away.

"Calidi and Ellris, I need you two to secure the hanger," Sophia commanded her servants.

The two members of the royal guard turned and left.

Chapter 29- The Explosion

Denise and Surge had been following Greenbreath who had separated from Baldassara. They watched as Greenbreath drew a pen-like object from his pocket and pressed the back button. A small gray stick, one millimeter in diameter, extended from the tip of the object. He jabbed the tiny stick into his wrist.

"What's he doing?" Denise looked on in discomfort.

"The current nick-name is blight sticks." Surge drew the revolver from his jacket. "Get Kira on the line. Once that stuff takes effect, I won't be able to take him on without a proper weapon."

Denise and Surge were thrown to the floor at the very moment of an explosion.

Greenbreath's now glowing turquoise eyes locked onto them.

"You're that bounty hunter." Greenbreath charged at them.

Surge dragged Denise up. He drew his mechanical revolver, firing as they jumped out of Greenbreath's way. The first shot stuck Greenbreath's shoulder and the second hit his lower torso, but third bullet merely shattered upon activation of his personal energy shield.

Greenbreath slammed into Surge, pinning him against the wall.

Knowing a pointblank shot would penetrate the force-field, Surge attempted to point the gun against Greenbreath's skin. But the drug-empowered man threw the bounty hunter over his shoulder, slamming him into the floor.

Denise kept firing in vain as the man charged at her, grabbing her by the neck. She pressed the tip of her gun against his wrist and fired her last bullet into his arm, shattering the blight stick.

Greenbreath dropped her on the ground and staggered back, gripping his wounded wrist. The contained chemical now surged through his veins.

The drug lord collapsed on the floor.

Denise coughed several times as she rubbed her bruised neck. She made her way over to Surge as he staggered up.

"Surge!" called the voice of Ray from his handheld. "Surge, are you there?"

"Yah, ow." He slowly pulled out his pocket computer. "We're

going to need to pick up on Greenbreath. What is it?"

"That explosion has sent the entire auction towards the main star in this system," Ray recounted. "Karl's headed towards the bridge in hopes of getting out of the way of that star. He wants you to meet up with him."

"Bloody pirate. Why doesn't he just leave on his ship?"

"The *Lady Eris* and most of the larger ships were knocked out by something similar to the recoil of the *Crimson Blade's* main weapon and were scattered in the explosion. The smaller ships in this hanger seem to be functional but we're locked in here."

"Can't you blast out?"

"Not without our main weapon, which will leave us dead in the water. And the other ships that would be freed wouldn't be enough to evacuate this place. I am also not sure if there'd be any force-fields to hold us back from the vacuum."

"So once the hanger's opened, those ships will be on their way without us."

"Pretty much, I'll keep an eye on things here."

"Send out a drone with weapons." Surge turned to their fallen enemy. "Have it pick up Greenbreath and stuff him in a cargo crate."

Chapter 30- The Caped Armor

Karl found himself in some kind of an armory. Standing with its arms crossed was a suit of armor with an underlying gold frame. It was overlaid with armor which resembled frosted glass. While certainly taller that the average man, the armor was nowhere near the height and mass of the Evlon armor he had encountered.

A long cape hung from its shoulders.

"You think this power armor could handle an Evlon Inquisitor or a Lrakian?" Karl looked under the cape to see two-rod like objects extending vertically from the upper back. The barrel of a rifle defined one end and the other had a sword grip. The rifle barrel was on the right and sword grip was on left.

"It's a gamble," Travis explained. "Sanwell claims to have found it in a hollowed out asteroid where it must have been lost for at least a millennium. The armor itself seems to be a mix of tech matching that of the Neith who left the original Lecaran homeworld before the Neith Empire and some pieces of tech that seem more advanced than our own."

"And the Evlon would claim it was from the Elders," Karl stated.

"That means I get to claim it." Lightening jumped on the right pauldron, sinking his claws into the cape. "Now I must ask why it isn't a giant lion instead of a human."

"The style is similar to the ceremonial armors worn in the Neith Empire. However, I believe most of them were still functional for combat." Sophia walked around, examining the armor. "It could work for armored boarding parties but those tend to be lighter and favor thrusters in the event of a hull breach."

"I think it could be a relative," said another voice.

Everyone turned to the doorway where the Oracle floated in.

"Karl, what's that?"

"Behold." The Oracle voice switched to its deep dramatic settings "I am the Oracle of the Great Elder-"

"Enough with that." Lightening looked up at the machine as though it were a dinner plate. "Have you brought supper?"

The Oracle lowered itself to the floor, and a small hatch

opened containing dried slices of meat. The food was immediately devoured by the tabby.

John and Travis looked on in shock over the interaction between feline and robot.

"Well, I guess it's worth a shot." Karl turned to Sophia. "Did you want to do it?"

"No. I expect you to handle most of the fighting." Sophia pressed down on a button inside the collar of her dress and the gown shrank down to a less formal and less cumbersome garment with slits on each leg for maneuverability. "I'll supervise your conquest."

"As his feline caretaker, supervising Karl's activity is my responsibility."

Karl pulled off his cape and sickle sword, handing them to Sophia. The armor's breastplate opened and its helmet slid back allowing Karl to step into the powersuit. The torso closed and the helmet folded over his head. The darkness inside the helmet was soon replaced with a heads up display and crosshairs for targeting enemies.

Sophia took Karl's cape and draped it on her shoulders, merely carrying the sheath khopesh in her right hand.

"You two better arm yourselves." Now armored, Karl turned towards his old classmates.

Travis and John did as instructed, each grabbing a plasma carbine and crystal sword. The group of six humanoids and a cat exited the armory on route to the bridge.

As they turned a corner, a couple in white and yellow appeared in front of them. The sword attached to Karl's armor instantly folded down to his left hand. A thin blue edge surrounding a black blade stuck a sword of plasma.

Momentarily Karl recognized the man as Prince Alec, who stood guarding Yuki. Karl lowered his weapon but did not halt his action, seeing as how Alec failed to do so.

"What is the meaning of this?" Alec had his sword ready to defend. "First, my guard is attacked. Second, I've lost contact with my flagship, and now you lot show up."

"There was an explosion along with an attack by what appeared to be Blood Terrans." Sophia stood behind Karl in a position where Alec could see her but not be able to strike her without going through Karl. "This ship is about to ram into a blue sun and we have to change course or get off of here before that happens."

"The other ships were knocked out and can't get to us now." Karl deactivated the charge-cutter and his helmet slid back. "We're headed towards the bridge to see if we can change course."

Alec switched off his weapon and plasma dissipated, revealing a metal rod which quickly retracted into the hilt. The crossguard of the young prince's weapon folded together where the blade had been.

"I guess I'm with you, then." Alec let go of Yuki's hand.

"There you are, Alec," called a voice in the direction from which the Titan prince had come.

Prince Ulai appeared down the hall gripping a short single edged transparent sword in his right hand.

"I see you're still alive." Alec turned to Ulai.

"Of course," Ulai said. "You'd think I meet my end in a place like this?"

"Can we not start an argument that leads to a chess game?" Lightening began bathing. "I'd like to be able to eat again before this life ends."

"That some kind of attack drone?" Ulai took notice of the Oracle.

"I am not some mere drone."

"No, he can't attack anything."

"So it's just some mechanical pet."

"I'll have you know I'm the most advanced artificial intelligence in the known galaxy."

"Enough about the useless robot, if you are still loyal to the old empire you will join us in redirecting this ship."

Chapter 31- Confrontation

The doors to the bridge slid open. Charles Sanwell stood at the main control console of the ship.

A circle of gavels rose from Charles' belt, surrounding him.

"You think you can stop us with your decorative holograms?" Karl pointed his sword at Sanwell.

"Captain, those are corporeal," Miss Holo informed.

The swarm of gavels orbiting around Charles Sanwell flew at them. Karl slashed three of them.

Sophia opened fire with her wrist gun, blasting two of the flying objects.

Karl cut the head off one gavel only to be hit by another, launching him into a wall.

"It is advisable not to let them hit you," Miss Holo interjected. "They seem to have micro gravity fields."

"Would have been nice to know that earlier." Karl staggered back up.

Sanwell drew his basket-hilted broadsword, and the sword turned red upon activation.

"So this was your plan! Offer up this ship to the highest bidder and then destroy it and flee with the profit." Sophia took aim at Charles.

"I'll admit that the idea was really Claymore's. My original plan was to allow the sale to be complete and then come back in a few months with a counter to this weapon. Sadly, while we were able to come up with a way of incorporating shields to resist the discharge, I was the one who discovered the deterioration of the artifact, which we incorporated into the ship's structure. The weapon would have failed after a couple more uses, which could have resulted in a burnout or possible self-destruction of the entire ship. So it was decided that the best option was to crash the thing into the nearby star in time for the patrons to be able to escape."

"So you never intended to kill the rich and powerful?" Alec still had his weapon angled towards Charles.

"No, the ships were never supposed to decouple from the auction-"

"Disposing of the other ships was a necessary act on our part." Kordova entered the room followed by his companion now clad in the Evlon battle armor, which had been on display earlier. "Once this ship is ours we shall begin our liberation of the Sol system from the false races and traitors to humanity."

"You missed the part where he said the super weapon was going to break." Lightening scratched his ear.

"All this for a piece of junk I stumbled across on an alien planet." Charles looked around for his chance to flee. "And you people really believe it is the key to exacting the will of your gods?"

"The Elders were more than just mythical wish granters," said the bearded man in blue robes. "They were the ones who seeded earth in order to ensure the ultimate race to inherit their legacy."

"And you still needed to reverse engineer our technology. Without us you wouldn't have made it out of your own solar system." Sophia's plasma coil was still in gun mode and began collecting energy at the tip. "My people were the ones who had power over the stars a millennium before yours could even touch its own moon."

"Now, now." Lightening stood up. "You’re both equally inferior under me, and your only happiness will come from your servitude to the Great Cat Empire under my benevolence. Now go get me a can of tuna."

"We would have developed naturally and discovered our destiny through our own power." Kordova paid no heed to the cat’s statement.

"And I'm being ignored." Lightening turned around and walked away. "Karl, Sophia, I don't think you should be associating with these sort of people."

"I'd very much like to not associate with them." Karl activated his charge cutter.

The Evlon warrior drew the hilt of a bladeless sword with his right hand. A long slender rod with a triangular tip extended from the center of the hilt. A pair of red beams streaked from the hilt of the sword to the triangular tip as the Inquisitor charged at Karl.

The two swords of the armored warriors struck each other. The edge of Karl’s longsword shattered and the black blade melted against the red plasma. As the antique sword failed, Karl jumped out of the way. Sophia tossed Karl his standard weapon and slashed the left knee of his enemy's armor.

The armored enemy struck Karl's helmet with his left fist. The inquisitor readied his weapon to finish the incapacitated Karl.

A charged shot fired from Sophia's plasma coil struck the left eye of the Evlon warrior's helmet. Half blinded, the Evlon turned towards Sophia, who frantically fired several weaker shots. She switched her weapon into a plasma blade upon activation deflecting the plasma claymore.

Ulai's charge cutter turned green upon engagement and he jumped at the inquisitor, stabbing though the thin armor of the right gauntlet.

The Evlon warrior knocked him aside with his left arm.

Karl slowly rose back up with his khopesh in his left hand and the remaining half of the longsword in his right. He dropped the damaged sword, the gun mounted under the right shoulder folded up and sent a white blast into the Evlon warrior. The discharged weapon detach itself from the armor, slamming onto the floor.

John tossed a second longsword to Karl. It turned yellow-gold upon activation, as the Evlon warrior just stood there motionless.

"The target in question is no longer conscious." A projection of Miss Holo appeared inside Karl's helmet.

"Kordova and Charles also seem to have also run away." Lightening appeared from his hiding place and jumped on Karl's shoulder.

They made their way to the control panel. Karl placed his handheld on the panel linking Miss Holo with the ship's computer.

"Oracle," Miss Holo's voice came from the console. "I will need assistance with this."

"Okay, let me see what I can do." The crystals orbiting the Oracle turned orange.

"Were you able to stop it?"

"Well, do you want the good news or the bad news?" the Oracle asked.

"Well, the ship is no longer headed for a star, however…" Miss Holo appeared on screen before Karl could respond.

"However what?" Sophia asked.

"The core of the ship's super weapon seems to have replaced itself with an unstable dimensional rift that seems to be slowly pulling the ship apart from the inside."

"How long have we got?"

"An hour, maybe one and a half."

Karl's handheld beeped.

"Captain Sabers!" Ray's voice beamed over the device. "I've received word all three of your pirate ships should arrive once they get their faster than light drives back online. But that may take around three hours. Also, there's a multitude just outside the hanger. We've got the corridors locked but I don't know how long that will last."

Chapter 32- The Escape

Kira took Greenbreath's legs and B-10 took his shoulders. The pair carried them towards the hanger.

A small drone had been deployed from the *Crimson Blade* carrying the bounty hunter's weapons, which seemed not to have much use at the moment.

Surge reattached his katana to his left hip and his revolver to his right.

"And you didn't send my weapons along?" Denise glared at the object.

"It wasn't considered essential this time." Ray's voice transmitted from the drone. The handle of a compact plasma cutter extended from the drone. "This should be enough for the moment. You two should just focus on getting back to the ship so we can get out of here."

Denise reluctantly took the basic tool in her hand, which emitted a foot-long purple beam upon activation.

The two bounty hunters turned to follow the drone back to the ship when Surge saw a familiar figure out of the corner of his eye.

"So it looks like it's time for a rematch." Surge turned to Baldassara standing there in the corridor.

"Surge, we have to get out of here, we already have Greenbreath captured." Denise pulled on the bounty hunter's arm trying to get him to come with her.

"Why stop now when we could have two lords of the Syndicate? Think what a blow that would be to them and the reward we could get." Surge gripped the bronze hilt of his katana.

"You should listen to your woman, bounty hunter." Baldassara activated his charge-cutter turning the scimitar violet. "The Syndicate will find a suitable replacement for Greenbreath. I see no reason for us to fight."

"Well I do." Surge's blade turned blue as it left its scabbard, with the bounty hunter charging at Baldassara.

Baldassara curved sword blocked the katana.

"There you are," said another man's voice.

They both turned to see King Bob walking towards them with

a grin on his face. Covering each of his forearms were a pair of gauntlets with crystal blades extending from the knuckles of each hand.

"Now where is that pride defector of yours?" King Bob's wrist blades turned red.

"I think we should settle this another time." Baldassara stepped back from Surge.

"I hate the idea of agreeing with you but..." Surge stepped back, readying himself for an attack from either King Bob or Baldassara. "I'll assume he's not on your side."

"Sadly no." Baldassara turned his full attention towards King Bob. "While you were passed out from the end of our last duel, our attempted alliance broke down when he threatened my niece."

The Lrakian man slashed at Surge, who jumped out of the way.

Baldassara swung his sword at the Lrakian warlord. Bob twisted the sword out of the crime lord's hand before slashing him in the side.

The mouth of Surge's dragon hilt snapped open and fired a series of micro-warheads at King Bob.

Surge spotted Baldassara clutching his wound, the yellow blood seeping through his clothing. He retrieved his scimitar before dashing past Denise and Surge.

King Bob stepped through the smoke with his arms crossed in front of his head and torso.

A seat of bulkhead doors slammed shut, separating the bounty hunters from King Bob.

"We don't know how long that will hold," Kira's voice said over Surge's handheld.

Red blades pierced the bulkhead door and it slowly slid down. Surge pulled back the hammer of his gun and aimed it at the door separating them from their enemy.

Bolts of electricity followed the projectile as it left the barrel. The doors bent away from them as the bullet passed through its target.

Denise and Surge exited a corridor leading into the hanger where they saw Karl and Sophia running along a catwalk followed by two other Terran men, a Terran woman in a white dress carried by a

Titan officer, along with a Neith man limping behind them.

Karl looked down to see the two priests standing across from Claymore and Sanwell. Approaching Claymore and Sanwell were Kordova and the woman who had lost her right arm to Karl.

Adjacent to the platform was a small triangular craft with three wings and a pair of Evlon Lancer.

On each side of the Lancer's cockpit was a gun with three prongs around it. Extending from behind the pilot's seat were two angled rods attached to a pair of small triangular wing engines.

"Now you're going to provide us with the location of the rest of those victims of alien oppression."

"Well, I am sure we can provide you with the location as well for that price you were offering to us at the auction." Claymore smirked as he pulled out his handheld. "Sanwell and I are the only ones who know their location. Despite what you people claim, you simply need those lost Terrans to be the manpower you lack."

Kordova's comrade took aim at Claymore, but was quickly halted by the old man.

Claymore took the disk and held it in front of Charles, who scanned it with a red monocle.

"It's safe." Charles confirmed with one glance. Claymore placed the disk inside his coat and the heads of the auction turned towards their escape ship.

Three missiles were launched from one of the silver spacecrafts, which had escorted Kordova and his companion. The first warhead was struck by the beam from the shuttle and exploded into a bright sphere. But the second pierced the shuttle's main engine and the vessel was pulled back, drifting into the pyramid ship's superstructure. With the target apparent elimination, the last missile disarmed and return to its launching tube. Karl looked upon the site in horror at the destruction that befell the parts that have been with him just mere moments ago.

"We've got to help them." Denise turned to her brother.

"Surge, Alec-"

"That's Your Highness, Prince Alec," the Terran prince interrupted.

"Get them to your ship and be ready to blast the hanger open."

"You can't just put us on the bus." Lightening jumped onto Karl's shoulder.

"This armor is airtight and has an oxygen recycler. Do you want to be present when those doors open into space?" Karl's helmet turned to the cat.

Lightening jumped into Sophia's arms.

"What have you to gain by this?" yelled Father Abraham. The old priest turned to the woman in the red uniform. "You…"

Without warning, Kordova's companion raised her gun and fired two green shots at Father Abraham before taking aim at Father Gabriel.

Remembering Tut's actions on Tau Ceti, Karl, with the aid of the powered armor, lept down onto the cockpit of the Lancer. Slashing open the canopy he pulled out the pilot and took control of the fighter.

"Now for you, abomination," said Kordova's companion

Before the companion had a chance to fire a shot at the young priest, Karl knocked the catwalk with the small spacecraft, causing the green plasma bolt to miss the priest.

The other craft fired on Karl's Lancer destroying the right-hand gun.

"It pains me to destroy one of our own craft to purge a race traitor." Kordova's voice came through the intercom in the Lancer. "But I guess it's the only way to put an end to you."

A pair of yellow blue particle beams fired at Kordova's Lancer.

The guns of Kordova's craft swung out on a pair of mechanical arms, which returned fire at the *Crimson Blade*.

Seeing his enemy distracted, the left-hand gun of Karl's Lancer swung out on a mechanical arm and fired a red beam straight into Kordova's cockpit.

Father Gabriel pulled Father Abraham over his shoulder. The cargobay doors on the *Crimson Blade* opened catching the two priests.

"Attention! All those not currently in a ship, please exit to outer ring or risk being sucked out into space." Karl aimed the main gun of his Lancer at the hanger door. "All armed ships prepare to depart."

A purple energy beam fired from the Lancer's main gun and a volley of missiles and energy beams followed the first strike. The hanger doors were blasted apart by the ships inside. The ships launched into space as every molecule of air was pulled from the hanger.

Karl scanned the collapsing pyramid ship from the cockpit of his Lancer.

"Surge." Karl flew the Lancer towards the *Crimson Blade.* "We're going to have to blast the connectors between the core and the outer rim."

A red joystick with a glass trigger rose from the floor in front of Surge's chair. The curved wings of the *Crimson Blade* swung open and red particles began collecting at the bow.

Surge squeezed the trigger. A wide red beam of glowing particles shot from the bounty hunter's vessel, cutting away the structures connecting the ring to the pyramid. The *Crimson Blade* remained active long enough to take out the connections on each side of the pyramid.

The lights usually illuminating the *Crimson Blade* flickered out and the small ship became dead in space.

"Why would you have a weapon that shuts down the entire ship every time you use it?" Sophia pulled out her handheld to use as a light.

"Not much that we can do in that case." Surge put his hands behind his head and leaned back in his chair. "It's hardwired into the frame of this ship, and you could even argue that it is the ship."

"So it was built out of some random alien super weapon." Lightening walked around the bridge rubbing his scent anywhere he could. "These aliens need to take better care of where they leave their toys."

"Weren't you saying that you were the owner of the ancient super weapons?" Sophia rolled her eyes in the darkness towards the sound of the cat.

"I can't be held responsible for the actions of another cat."

"What seems to get knocked out is the modern components that were built around the original gunship." Ray jumped up from his seat and left for the engine room.

A white and brown triangular ship appeared in a bright flash. The unknown ship fired several cables into the broken ring section of the auction ship. The blue tractor beams activated, pulling the gold ring away from the black pyramid. The ring section was freed from the collapsing pyramid, which slowly folded into a white light at its center, then vanished.

"We are the Barley People," a voice introduced. "We were asked by a Mr. Sanwell to arrive in this system but were sadly delayed."

Chapter 33- The Departure

Several of the larger cruisers and space yachts now docked with the Barley People's ship and the remains of the vessel that once hosted the Auction of Worlds.

"Well, Sir Karl, the Titan Empire owes you a debt. How much of a debt, though, is in proportion how much my death would have caused grief to my parents, grandmother, and relatives who wouldn't have benefited from my demise. And a considerable amount of tax money has been saved by delaying my funeral. As thanks I shall ensure the safety and prosperity of my future bride and your people who have now become my subjects." Prince Alec crossed his arms.

Weren't you going to do that anyway, when you were bidding for Yuki's hand in marriage? Karl wondered.

"I appreciate it. And what about a possible alliance with Sophia?" Karl put his hands in his pockets.

"Well, I can submit a request to my father who can present it to the Great Houses who will have to vote on it. Then the Chancellor will have to approve it and then it should go well, so long as my grandmother does not pass judgment against it. Also, I'll forget that incident where your ship took off with my kill."

"All right, I get it." Karl rolled his eyes. "Red tape."

"Do you really want to go through with this?" Denise cried, hugging Yuki. "I'm sure I could convince Surge or Karl to let you join their crews."

"I have to do this." Yuki smiled looking to Brittany. "Deep space is no place for their little ones." She gazed at Prince Alec. "What greater achieve…I mean sacrifice is there than to become the bride of a prince for your people?"

A sense of jealousy overcame Denise. *I'm only a bounty hunter's cook and Yuki has just became engaged to a prince. Not to mention, Karl might as well be married to Princess Sophia, the way she runs things.*

Denise calmed herself, remembering it was her duty to bring them all to Jesus.

Yuki soon joined Prince Alec as he returned to his flagship. John and Brittany followed the royal couple.

"Not going?" Karl glanced over to Travis, who was still standing around them.

"I thought I would stick around here and see the Galaxy." Travis pulled his hand out of his pocket and waved at Zrela who had arrived with the rest of Karl's crew. "John's has the coordinates of the other students and since he's a family man now, he will be better off settling down on a new planet."

"So how many went along with the idea of being the last of humanity and needing to repopulate?" Karl remembered that they had all been paired up on the mothership based on calculated genetic compatibility.

"I think at least two thirds of the girls embraced it and half of them became mothers right away." Travis looked around at some of the young women in the room with them. "While the remaining third split between those who never wanted children or were wanting to maintain their purity for true love. My supposed selected partner was one of the latter."

"Saving a Martian Priest instead of protecting Her Highness." Calidi walked up behind them.

"Sophia was already on Surge's ship." Karl turned to the older bodyguard. "She was safer there than with me and the Lancer. You can always take things up with her."

"If the space princess is mad she can just deny him her presence." Lightening jumped on Karl's shoulder.

Calidi left, ignoring the comments of the feline.

Karl glanced over at the approaching Isabella and Selina, who had been among the servants stranded on the ship during the disaster.

"Captain Sabers." Selina looked at Karl dead on. "We humbly request the opportunity to serve as members of your crew until such time as our masters can be found!"

"I'm sorry to say this but I saw their ship fall into that rift." Karl felt sympathy for the two girls who had likely gone from cared-for property to liberated and destitute.

"I know Master Ashley has to be alive." Isabella stared at him with her blue eyes.

"We believe that rift may have functioned as a wormhole and their shuttle merely was lost in space and not destroyed." Selina pulled back her right sleeve, revealing the gem in her slave bracelet. "The bracelet would have totally deactivated if the control rod had been destroyed but it is still functional."

And I thought I might be rid of Claymore. Karl glanced over at Sophia. "I'll have to consult with a few of my crew before making that decision."

"Trust me, Karl, a harem of alien women may seem like a good idea, but it is more trouble than it is worth." Lightening rubbed his face against Karl's.

Karl found Sophia with Father Gabriel and Prince Ulai. The latter was flat on a powered stretcher.

Prince Ulai was transported to his ship before Karl met with them.

"Sophia, I have to talk to you about some requests for new crewmen." Karl glanced back to see Travis chatting with Selina and Isabella.

"Looks like you're not the only one with a xenofetish." Lightening jumped down.

"You know the Worshiping Kitty looks like you." Sophia looked down at the feline. "We could just have it act as a replacement."

"I would never stoop to acknowledge such a creature." Lightening raised his tail and turned to leave.

"I have performed last rites on Father Abraham. I will have to accompany his body to Mars for burial, but you have my permission to use the chapel located on our ship before I depart," said Father Gabriel.

"Permission for what?" asked Karl.

Sophia grabbed Karl's arm and dragged him towards the Martian ship.

Chapter 34- Almost Back to Normal

Having left Denise to say goodbye to her friends and brother, Surge had returned to the galley of the *Crimson Blade*. With her gone for the moment, he might be able to have his traditional meals in peace.

Surge pulled on the refrigerator door but it did not budge. He tapped the screen fearing Denise may have set a password.

"Access denied," responded the refrigerator interface. "Surge, please eat healthy."

A cucumber rolled out of a slot in the fridge.

"How am I supposed to eat this?" He picked up the green object and stared at it. "Maybe with some tuna ice-cream dip."

"Meow."

He turned around to see the black tail-less cat sitting on the galley table.

"Here you can have this." Surge pointed the cucumber at the feline.

Emerald turned her nose up, jumped off the table, and trotted out the door.

"You're right. It must be poison." He tossed the green vegetable on the counter.

A Lecaran woman with long wavy metallic gold hair was seated on a steel throne. Her torso was clad in a form-fitting cuirass of frosted glass plates with a silvery dress split at each thigh, and on her left hand was a black gauntlet with blade-like fingers.

"You were fortunate, Your Highness." Ishtana bowed, still dressed in her black cape with gold trim. "Had your ship not been delayed, you would have been in immense danger."

"Yes. But I had hoped to confirm the authenticity of the woman the Neith Federation thinks is my sister."

"I assure you she is genuine." Ishtana pulled a yellow jewel designed to change color in proximity to any royal descendants. "She appears to have gained some allies, among which is a Terran whom she seems to enjoy dressing up. The only nobles present at the auction appeared to be Ulai of Talon and former Grand Duke Baldassara, who seems to have turned to a life of crime."

"A Terran!"

"I suppose we will have to find her a proper suitor."

"No, if she marries someone that low below her station it could prevent her from becoming a threat to my future rule."

Dalia looked at the Lrakian positioned face down in his cell. A sheet of weapons grade glass acted as a barrier between them.

"The gravity should keep him down for the moment, it's certainly enough to crush one of us." The first officer stood beside her. "Theoretically, we shouldn't ever need to cover the cell."

"I'd rather have something to stall him if the gravity field fails."

Dalia watched on as King Bob attempted to raise himself.

"Mark my words." The intense gravity pulled King Bob to the floor. "My pride will come for me and once I am free you will know my wrath."

"If you'd calm that rage of yours, we could discuss the terms of your freedom." The admiral turned to her officers. "What of the other prisoners?"

"The old man is dead, the red blood male and female are both still alive for the moment but have lost a few parts. Should we dispose of them?"

"Not yet. Let's see if we can make use of them." Dalia walked along to another cell, which held a shackled pair of Terrans. A woman missing her right arm and a man without a right hand or left leg. "Perhaps we can reprogram the three of them. Otherwise I believe memory sealing is in order."

I've never been with a Lrakian before. it will be interesting to see how they compare to the men of other races.

Dalia smiled in anticipation.

Chapter 35- The Knighting

Karl and Sophia stood alone in the Cathedral.

"I suppose now is as good a time as any." Sophia looked at the altar.

"For what?"

Sophia dragged him by the wrist toward the altar, stopped in from of him, turning back towards him.

"Kneel."

Karl did as instructed and Sophia raised his sword in her left hand.

"Do you swear in the sight of God to protect and serve the Neith Empire and her royal family with your life under pain of death?"

"I swear."

Sophia tapped Karl's left shoulder once and his right twice.

"To Her Highness Sophia Vearis Rubyeyes for as long as I live."

"I knight thee, Sir Captain Karl Sabers." She dropped to her knees and kissed him on the lips. "Knight of Second Neith Empire."

Lightening walked into Karl and Sophia's cabin alone, ready for a well-deserved catnap. There on Karl's bed he found the Worshiping Kitty sitting there ready to please its master. He jumped on the bed and glared daggerously at the toy.

"All threats to my kingdom must be dealt with swiftly." He swatted the fake cat off the bed and curled up for a night's rest.

There would be much tribute in the form of tuna required in the morning.

Galactic Guide

Neith Empire/Federation

Venus– Current capital world of the Neith Federation and former Neith Empire. After being xenoformed by the Lecarans, the aliens took up residence in the upper atmosphere where they built and converted starships into sky cities. The surface cannot be accessed without pressure resistant ships. And in some cases, powered armor similar to what would be used to protect against the pressure of the deep-sea on earth. Banishment to the surface is every citizen's greatest fear.

Earth– Stolen from humanity by those of the Neith Empire. Most of the remaining humans exist as second class citizens or slaves to the ruling aliens. Antarctica remains the only Non-Lecaran continent and exists as an enclave of the Koal.

Mercury– While the closest to the sun, enclosed habitable territories were established on each of the poles, which grew out of the original mining outposts.

The Mars Imperium

Mars– The home world of the Martian Imperium. The completely terraformed world with a population consisted of those descended from North American and Chinese astronauts. The two groups of national colonists were previously in a semi-cold war up until the fall of Earth after which the two sides united under Catholicism. Capital city of this planet is Aries and is home to new Vatican City. Protestant religion is legalized but 90% of the population is Catholic and the area is often considered to be the puppet empire of the papacy.

Ceres– A dwarf planet located in the asteroid belt. The planet itself is covered entirely by an ocean with all residents living predominantly within an artificial ring surrounding the planet. The ring is held in place with four towers driven into the planet's rocky core.

Tau Ceti System– Martian controlled system with an Earthlike Terraformed world.

Titan Empire– The founders of which chose to hide themselves within the orbit of Saturn after the fall of Earth. Saturn's Moon Titan was conquered and later terraformed by a group claiming descent from all the ancient ruling families of Europe. They became the Protestant power in the galaxy following the second reformation. The current monarch is Her Majesty Kaiserin Alexandria Victoria.

The Jovian states

Europa– Considered one of the wealthiest and most powerful of the states surrounding Jupiter. While there is a small percentage of nomads and scientists living in ice structures on the surface, the bulk of the population live in upside down cities that are anchored underneath the frozen crust of the planet within the moon's vast oceans. Europa currently has aquatic life which provides the inhabitants with an abundance of food. It is still unconfirmed if the lifeforms that exist in the oceans are natural or were placed there by the Koal who once occupied that moon.

Callisto– A tidal locked colonized Moon, often seen as Europe's rival for control of Jupiter's sphere. The underground water of the planet has been brought up and the planet is covered in a series of circular lakes formed by the flooded craters of the moon. Being outside the radiation of Jupiter, its population has the least amount of biological resistance to radiation.

Ganymede– Has the largest population of Jupiter's moons but also has the least amount of resources so is also almost completely dependent upon trade. As the largest moon in the solar system, it was once intended to be the greatest of humanity’s first set of colonists. The original colony fell to ruin after the fall of Earth.

Io– The most heavily irradiated of Jupiter's moons, exists almost in its entirety as a volcanic desert. The moon was never intended to be an actual colony but rather as an outpost for resource gathering from Jupiter and its smaller moons. Once cut off from Earth, the isolated workers formed a self-sufficient nation around that moon. Resources are managed by a totalitarian dictatorship, which is considered by many to be a necessary evil in order for population survive on the desolate moon.

The Race of Extraterrestrial Origin

*Lecaran/*Neith– A race that is structurally similar to mankind, but have some differing elements in their make up, resulting in yellow blood. Their eyes come in shades of red, yellow, and violet. They have metallic colored hair which turns black as they age. Some believe their resemblance to humans is due to an artificial origin, while others believe it to be a sign of a Divine Creator.

Koal– Born on dark low gravity cryo worlds. To survive on warmer worlds the Koal encase themselves in a form of power armor that keeps their bodies cool. The oldest space faring of the known races, many believe their current humanoid form is a result of manipulating their own genes.

Lrakian– An artificial race engineered by the Koal around a thousand or so years ago. Their ears resemble those of cats and wolves, with the rest of their bodies having a Terran or Lecaren appearance. The race is split into two different categories, those with cat-like tail are known as Pride Lrakian and those with wolf-like tails are known as Pack Lrakians. They have no original homeworld and no recognized governments, but are valued as mercenaries. Pride leaders are referred to as kings.

Also published by Ruskras Corner

Science Fiction
3748 A.D. The Return of the Cat by Carl S. Kralich

"Humorous young adult science fiction. Hilarious tale of princesses, pirates, and a talking cat. For adults and young adults, male and female. Romance and gallantry in the stars." It's the year 3748. Humans have long been separated from Earth and cats thought extinct. But felines endure and a young history student gets caught up in enthralling events when his evangelical-minded sister gets in trouble and he has to travel the universe to find her, meeting princesses and pirates along the way as he transforms into Karl Sabers- Space Knight Adventurer!

Historical Literature Fiction
The Mystery of the Missing Persons by Deborah DR Kralich

A museum piece, must read for history fans..." Covers the years 1963 - 1967 and chronicles the tremendous changes in American society in that short time. The book contains a complete mystery actually written in the 1960s by a 10 year old. Enjoyable in itself, Victoria's mystery strikes a humorous contrast to the tense times and gives unique insight into the inner workings of minds of children.

Murder Mysteries by Deborah DR Kralich
The Mystique Woven in Our Land

Historical fiction with mystery and romance, set in 1792. Vanishings in Kentucky spark fears of government conspiracies combined with the supernatural. An experiment in tolerance and unprecedented freedom for women unexpectedly yields chaos. Daughter of the general, only 17, Lantern finds herself at the center of excitement as the town prepares an elaborate celebration. Her admirer, Major Plate, a skeptical soldier with a detective's mind, suspects common criminality but he is shocked when he confronts spies instead of thugs and must plan a staged killing to bring out those invoking the black arts of evil to undermine the new republic.

Murder as the Organist Plays
"A mystery set in 1904 in old East Texas with many twist and turns." As the wedding music starts, the bride begins her long walk to the arms of her groom. But she will not finish the journey. The beautiful bride emerges stunned, blood on her dress. She stands alone, blood dripping from a dagger at her fingertips. Unknowing, his back to this scenario, the organist plays on... Only one man, flamboyant and mysterious, stands between her and a noose or an asylum. Turn of the Century picturesque East Texas is the setting for this mystery thriller with historical aspects. What happens next takes the reader on an exciting journey of mystery, love, and suspense with a completely twisted ending.

Lt. Plate in Sand Waves Mysteries
A series of traditional mysteries set in the 1980s including:

An Innovative Murder for the Season

"Great plot with many twists and interesting characters, not your usual group. 1980's technology limitations complicate the plot as does the socioeconomics of the time."...says one review.

"Nice larger 14 pt font for easy reading."

Complex characters and plot, early 1980s American Suburban setting, A good old fashioned book.

A massive flood threatens as the Christmas season dawns in the Houston/Galveston area. People living there don't expect a white Christmas but they hope for a dry Christmas. It is hot, humid and floodwaters everywhere have trapped people in inconvenient and dangerous situations. At a small specialty store in a high income community, a dozen or so people are trapped for 3 days and 2 nights. On the surface most appear to be strangers caught at random. Then there is a murder and it turns out the only real stranger among them is a detective whose presence is hardly coincidental.

The Ruler of the Toys

"An in depth mystery that explores social change in the 1980s while being highly entertaining. Part of a series but not necessary to read them in sequence. More serious and thought provoking than the first, still enjoyable in the tradition of old fashioned mysteries."

The world is changing in the 1980s and the new generation is having to cope with the legacy of the old. Elites would like to forget the social ills of the past and proclaim the new social order has arrived. But the boast is premature. Intolerance and prejudice are major factors in the murder of an innocent woman who should have been without an enemy in the world. Before he can expose the masquerade of the killer, Lt. Plate has to uncover and understand deep dark secrets of long vanished eras. Eager to delve into history with Lt. Plate, exploring superstitions and evils of ages gone by, is insurance agent Daphne Martin who has a secret agenda of her own. Plate and Daphne find sins of the past have long tentacles that reach far into their own times of the 1980s, and threaten to multiply in their future which, for the reader, is now. Before the end, this 1980s couple must make life and death choices in a world where good and evil have blurred and a wrong decision is fatal. Second in a series with the descendant of a 1900s law man and his insurance agent girlfriend.

A Kaleidoscope of Masquerades

"Miss the old fashion thriller mysteries that richly entertained? Then this book is for you! Stunning cover as well! Part of a series but not necessary to read them in sequence. This is the best so far!"
Climatic events at a 1983 masquerade ball are merely the beginning of a kaleidoscope of confusion and anarchy that threatens life and liberty of a society facing change and choices that will reverberate into the future known as now. The cost for a ticket is more than Lt. Sinclair Plate makes in a month as a police officer but he will be there on duty. Successful insurance agent, Daphne Martin, can afford a ticket but several others are planning to crash the party and steal the show. Fears for the safety of the guests take a backseat to concerns as to which politician or socialite will get to wear which costume. Little do they know the fates of past royals are intertwined with destinies of 1980s celebrities, as is the future direction of the country, in this historical fiction mystery featuring Lt. Sinclair Plate, descendant of a famous 1900s Texas lawman, combining forces with Daphne Martin, his insurance agent girlfriend. The fate of Plate and Daphne's relationship also hangs in the balance as Plate contemplates old and new women in his life and how any future with Daphne would impede his work in the present. They must also choose the direction of their lives. A mystery thriller set in 1983.

The Unknown Puppeteer

A killer stalks the wedding party!
On the eve of their marriage, Lt. Plate and Daphne must uncover a ruthless murderer or forfeit their chance for happiness for all time. Their fledgling romance began as sparks during a flood, simmered within a scandal, and caught fire amidst a storm of anarchy. Now it would only be justice if Lt. Plate and Daphne could enjoy a long and stress free engagement, then sail away into the sunset after a quiet wedding… Not meant to be. A chance at a dream Hollywood style ceremony pushes up their nuptial calendar, which would be fine if Plate also did not have to tend to security for a runaway princess bride, a Japanese VIP also claiming royal ties, a prominent movie producer staging a murder in Sand Waves, and then the surprise acquittal of an East Texas serial killer who murders on land and sea. With half his fellow officers taking off for sailing trips on Galveston Bay, and the chief busy trying to learn the new computer technology of the 1980s, Plate is left with only Grant Skaar, the youngest member of the force, as backup. Still Plate is coping, and Daphne is selling all parties involved as much insurance as she can, when suddenly everything has to take a backseat to an unimaginable tragedy within the police department. Fourth in a series of featuring the descendant of a famous Texas lawman and the woman he loves.

Available on Amazon and Kindle.

www.ingramcontent.com/pod-product-compliance
Lightning Source LLC
Chambersburg PA
CBHW072229190626
46809CB00017B/1661

* 9 7 8 1 9 4 2 5 4 2 1 5 5 *